Half Men

by Sandra Warren

Acknowledgements;

I dedicate this story to my dad John Jennings Warren and to my son, Patrick Neal; because of the close bond we all have. Patrick diligently edited this book for me. Cover design by Minnie Hernandez.

Chapter One

Raven did not know how really important she was. Sailing on a small ship with her brother in open ocean in the middle of a dark ocean was one thing. The fact that they were alone, could anyone or thing exist where they were. One constant thing was the fish. Every other day they would move their boat to a new spot to cast their nets. What bothered her was not the boat, nor the constant fishing. Seth, her brother, had been doing it long before she came around. When their parents died, she had to come and live with Seth. There was no one else. The one thing that did bother her occurred at night. Every night at three minutes past midnight, the march would take itself up again. The half men, only seen from the waist down, would march across her bedroom floor, from her door to the far corner of the room. As soon as they reached the corner the half men would vanish, like they were never there.

Nothing that she had ever seen or heard did not prepare her for this singularity.

Hiding in the alcove where she slept every night, she would look out the peephole her brother had made for her. The peephole was positioned so she could view the whole room, in case of brigands or pirates. It was not made for viewing wraiths from another dimension.

She decided then and there that she would speak to Seth about it before it got too dark outside. Raven knew her brother well. When the sky darkened after the sun went down, Seth could only be found in one spot. His pallet in the belly of the ship was where he would be. So, before any more time passed, she walked across the boat to the stairs that led down to where Seth was. She made sure to tread lightly so she could snatch the minutes from him.

Seth saw her as she approached him. She gave him a small start because Raven was an exact copy of their mother. For a second, he thought it was her, coming back to check on him, as she did in his dreams.

"I am sorry to bother you brother. I know that it is near your sleep time. Let me get to it quickly," Raven began to explain how she saw the half men every night at three strokes past midnight. She also pleaded with Seth to stay with her in her bedroom tonight, so he could see them too. Proving once and for all that she was not crazy.

After all was said and done, Seth agreed to stay with her tonight, but only until the half men were seen. He had to get up early, before Raven, so he could set the nets for the day's fishing. Grumbling all the way, he followed her up the stairs to the deck, checking the sails, to make sure they did not open up as they slept. He yanked at the anchor line as they passed.

Slowly, they both entered into Raven's bedroom.

"You should be glad that I agreed to come up here with you. I would soon be asleep if I was left alone," Seth grumbled with all the muster he could find. Raven looked quietly at her brother, knowing he was just saying this so she would respect his wishes from now on. She knew that he knew how important this was to her. He had observed her, many times, sitting on the top deck, deep in thought. She would tell him that she was watching for what they called painted fish, who were very toxic to be near, touch, or even eat. These fish did not swim in this part of the ocean, so he knew something large was weighing on her mind.

"Here Seth, you can sit opposite the peephole. It is about an hour until the half men show up, so we have a little time to discuss this," Raven said and slid the small door closed that curtained off her sleeping room. She then settled down beside her brother, patting his leg as she sat down next to him.

Seth was obviously perplexed.

"Why are you so crazy about these half men? Raven, you know they are just a myth, told by our parents to make us behave. You'd better eat all your dinner and get your bath or the half men will get you! You remember when Mom used to say that to us when Pop was out to sea, on this boat!"

All he could do was put his head down so Raven would not see his tears. She knew they were there.

"Listen, I think it is going to start soon. I hear the crunching sound that I always hear before it starts," Raven pointed to the peep hole, which was directed to see everything in her small room. She could hear the stamping of feet outside her door. Seth stretched his ear as far as he could to hear anything. Looking at Raven somehow made him believe that the singularity was beginning to form.

Seth looked hard into the peephole, not wanting to miss anything that he was to see. Slowly, by slowly, one and then another half man would appear before the bedroom door. All clad from the waist down in breeches, that covered their loins. Down the legs were leather lacing, none like which he had ever seen before. On their feet were leather thongs, lacing part way up to the ankles.

Of course, their upper parts, like the their torsos, arms, necks and heads could not be seen. It was mere vapor from the waist up. It took them a while to gather all together at the door. Seth counted the sets of legs, coming with twenty pair as a total.

He could not believe what he was seeing. Raven had been right all along!

They launched themselves one at a time in a slow canter. Seth noticed that they each had a different skin color. Some were black, some were brown, and so many other colors, he could not keep count. From the waist down, they were all dressed the same. What would tell where they came from would be located on the top half of their bodies. He wondered first, how they got exactly here. Second, why they were here, this particular spot. Unless the dimensional rift was skewed. He was aware of certain dimensions, adjacent to their earth, that were thousands of years behind them, evolutionary speaking. In others, there were those who far surpassed their own populations, as far as evolution was considered. This would take some study.

The last of the half men disappeared into the far corner of the room. Going to, or disappearing from life as they knew it. Seth and Raven both knew that this would be complicated to understand. Nonetheless, they would have to.

Raven looked at her brother's eyes, opened so large they looked like dinner plates. The light blue that they were almost disappeared into the white that surrounded them. His pupils were mere pin pricks in the middle. Reaching for the water bottle behind her, she poured him a cup, saying, "Here drink this slowly. It will go away in a while."

"What will go away?" Seth asked as he brought the cup up to his lips.

"The visions," Raven said as she looked away from her brother. To her, it seemed as if one of the half-men was stuck. Half in this world and half in what? She asked herself. Staring at what was visible, she touched her brother's leg.

"Seth, one of them is still here.

Look over there at the corner. Do you see it?"

Seth's eyes, as best they could, followed where his sister was pointing. In the far corner of the room, he could see the toe end of a foot, and what looked like a flapping rag above it. His eyes were much his own now,so he knew what he saw was right. After taking in a full view of the situation, he turned to his sister.

"What should we do?" He asked as he tried to still his shaking hands.

Raven took her brother's hands into hers. Slowly, she warmed them and stopped the shaking.

"We will have to address it together, Seth. Let us go over there very slowly, so we do not alarm the creature. I am not sure of what the creature is, and where it is from. One thing I am sure of, we have to find out."

The brother and sister got up together, opening the small alcove door to the main room. Raven could hear the shuffling of the creature's feet as it struggled to free itself from the corner.

"Do not hurt me, please. I have had enough anguish. Please help to free me so I can return to my incarceration," The creature spoke clearly, letting Raven and Seth know, without a doubt, that this creature might be of a human nature.

Walking side by side, Raven and Seth held each others hand, walking super slow towards the corner of the room. They could both see a mist covered outline over what would be the top part of the half man. The head of the man looked oddly shaped within the small pocket of fog that covered the top part of the creature. It looked almost animal like in how it was configured. Seth decided to take the first pitch.

"Uh, sir, um, half-man sir. Do you have a top half, by any chance? Is there a way we can see it, or even see you altogether? Our perception might not be the same as yours, so we must try and understand what we are dealing with. Can you get solid on top as you are on the bottom?"

The creature struggled within the mist about him. It looked as if he could not free himself enough for Seth and Raven to get a good look at him.

"I do not know if what I look like on top would be considerate to what you are used to. I am from a different earth than you. Where I am incarcerated is on still a different earth than this one and the one I come from. You are aware that there are at least twenty different earths in this galaxy alone, each having its own individual evolution. On my earth I was a scientist. When I tried to engineer a sentient life form, I was taken to a judicatory. After that I was put into incarceration on earth fifteen, across the galaxy from here."

"Then why do you and the others cross this room every night? My sister sees you and the others every night, at three minutes past midnight. Why the time and why here?

"Raven's black eyes flashed as her brother spoke to the creature.

The creature stammered in his thoughts. It appeared that he was not ready to tell all of his secrets. In a sheer point of decision the creature stepped out of the mist. His clothing was torn from being caught in the corner of the room. His left foot was bleeding from connecting with the wood of the corner. As he appeared to them, the siblings were astonished at what they saw. Only in picture books did they ever see a creature such as this.

The tall forehead, the full lips, large blue eyes staring at Seth and Raven, trying to relate to what everyone was seeing. The creature tried to smooth his bushy, unkempt hair.

"You are from the tenth earth. Mankind only went as far as the ones called "Neanderthal" after a valley where some ancient skeletons were found. We are on the ninth earth. Our humanity has physically evolved to what you see in front of you. Excuse me, but you speak so clear and intelligent. I did not expect that," Raven tried to look at the man, trying not to disrespect him.

"I am not as you understand. I love, think, grieve and see such as you both do. Do not judge me on how I look. What is within counts more that what is without," The man shifted his feet, because his left foot was bleeding so, that it needed a bandage or something even more to stop the course of the blood.

"I need some medical help, please. I gashed my left foot on a splinter of the wall. I feel that I have lost a lot of blood, can you help me please? I promise I will tell you more about my predicament as you help me. Fair deal, OK?"

It did not take them long to spring to action. Raven kept a competent medical kit in her small bedroom. She took it out, asking the man to sit down so she could kneel down and fix his wound. As she did this, the man looked at her intensely, as if trying to figure her out. He did not want her to take it in any way other than casual observation.

Within minutes, Raven's practiced hands had the wound cleaned and dried, bandaged not too tight, as to interfere with his blood circulation. While she was doing this, she was thinking of how different this man was from any other man she had ever seen. She saw and worked with Seth every day.

When they went to shore to sell their fish, she would look at the hard driven men, mending their nets, haggling for a good price for the fish they had brought. The women on shore were just as hard, from their lives, experiences and so forth.

Then she thought of her parents. Her mother with her darker than black hair and eyes. Her father with his red hair and bright blue eyes. Seth reminded her of their father. It was then that star like tears formed in both of her eyes, trickling slowly down her cheeks.

This show of emotion horrified the man. He reached to stop her tears from going down her cheek, "Lady, are you OK? Why are you crying? Is it something I did?" The man sat there dumbfounded at what he was witnessing.

Seth looked at the man, trying not to get upset. He really wasn't doing anything wrong, just commenting about Raven's situation.

It was the way that the man looked at his sister that bothered him.

"Do not get so close to my sister. On this earth we respect the boundaries, that each of us has set around our own selves. Please take your hand from her face."

The man was startled. No where he had ever been had anyone react that way. Instantly he took his hand down.

"I am sorry that I disrespected you, my dear Lady. I am a man from another earth, unaware of the right thing to do. I may look different than what you are used to, but that does not mean that I do not feel similar to you, within my heart."

Raven looked at the man with her liquid black eyes, still moist with tears.

"What is your name, sir. By what are you called?" Her eyes took in the situation for what it was worth. The man posed no threat to her.

She just wanted to understand the man, and, with that, she could find out the real story behind it.

"My name is Bernis. In my home language, it means "the man who is there." My Father named me, shortly before he died. My father was the high chief of my nation. The people that look like me are called "Narhas" by our culture, not the Neanderthal as you pointed to. We are a peaceful nation, not wanting to provoke any conflict of any kind. When the Waddis nation came and took over our nation, there was nothing we could do. My father had not picked an heir to his title. I am the youngest of four brothers, so the title would not be mine.

When the Waddis took over our nation, they put us to work in ways we were unfamiliar. The Waddis were well known on my earth, to be an intelligent race of men that used technology. The Narhas, on the other hand, had farms and raised fruit and vegetables for most of my planet. This was not enough for the Waddis. They took all the farmlands and gathered them into a coalition, answering only to the directors of the rule. The rest of the population was trained in various forms of technology. As myself, I was sent to a school to study. When I tried to create a sentient life form, I was deemed unfavorable, and sent to the mines. I do not know how long I was incarcerated. I do not even know what year it is, or even how old I am. I only know what I have told you, and that I am here."

Seth got up. It was nearly dawn, and he had to throw the nets to catch the fish that they would sell when they made it to land.

"Raven, will you be OK with Bernis while I handle the nets?" He said and started walking towards the door to the top deck.

Rachel looked at Bernis, then at Seth, " I think I will be fine. Do not forget, I have Tulli here beside me," she petted her dog to assure Seth, and Bernis to be on their best behavior.

As Seth went to the deck of the boat, he stooped to pick up the basket of nets that they would throw into the sea, bending to reach another basket to put by the rails, so they could throw the fish into it as they took them out of the net. This basket was very large, and he would need Raven's help to empty it into the frozen chest, where they would keep two or three days catch within it until they could go to shore. While he was doing this,he hoped that Raven and Tulli were OK. Against his better judgement he had left her alone with Bernis, or whoever he really was. he finished quickly so he could go back into Raven's quarters.

Approaching the stairs going down he could hear Raven laughing.

He had not heard her do that since their parents died. When he got down to the floor of the room, he saw the cause of the laughter. Bernis was trying to pet Tulli, but the dog wanted nothing to do with the stranger. He was running around the man so fast, no one could catch him. Seth sat on the bottom step, waiting for whatever else would happen.

Raven saw Seth sit down. She got up off of the floor, walking to the small stove they kept there to cook their meals. She took the coffee pot that was boiling on top of the stove, and poured her brother a cup of hot, black coffee. Taking it to him, he could see her black, liquid eyes were shining with happiness and laughter. Tulli had tired out of his escapade, sitting himself down on Bernis' lap. It was then, with the acceptance of the dog, that he could feel comfortable with this stranger.

"Would you like some coffee? I can put milk and a bit of sugar to make it taste better, "Raven held the cup towards Bernis, hoping he would at least, taste it.

Bernis took the cup, trying to balance the dog and the coffee so it would not spill. It looked strange to him as he held the cup under his nose. Coffee was for the Waddis only on his earth. He blew on the coffee to cool it off. After that he sipped the brew. It tasted wonderful to him. The first thing normal he had done in a long time.

"Thank you Raven, this is really good. My compliments to you," he said as he slowly enjoyed the coffee.

"It is OK, Bernis. I have more if you want it. I am going to start breakfast. Would you like a fried egg and some toast bread? I know you must be hungry."

Raven turned to work on the breakfast.

The eggs were soon sizzling in the pan. Seth cut the bread for them to toast.

The smells were intoxicating for Bernis. He had not smelled anything this good since he had left his earth for his incarceration. Even though there were many earths throughout the galaxy, many of the foods, languages,and customs were very similar. None the less,the man had a hard time accepting the kindness of this brother and sister. He began to weep. As he wept, little Tulli licked the tears as they fell off of his face.

Raven was balancing Bernis' plate and a another cup of coffee. She had managed to grab a towel, so Bernis could wipe his face and hands. The towel had been steeped in warm water, to make it extra comfortable. Kneeling down, she put the man's plate by his feet, the coffee cup beside it. Tulli would not leave his lap, so she wiped his face, handing him the towel so he could clean his hands.

When he was done, tears still flowed from his eyes. He looked up at Raven, "Thank you, my lady, helping a man such as myself. It has been a few years since anyone has been this kind to me. I appreciate all you and your brother are doing."

"It is OK Bernis. Seth and I were raised to treat others as we would treat ourselves. Our parents, bless them, were the most wonderful teachers in the world. Here, I will eat with you. Let me get my plate and I will keep you company as you eat. You know, Tulli might expect a tidbit or two. I guess you might already know," Raven said and laughed at the small dog sharing the man's plate. Seth brought her plate over, and some extra bacon and coffee. He sat down with them, finishing his coffee while he sat there.

"Bernis, would you like to help us bring in the nets? It's usually just Raven and myself.

Well, we do OK, but we could use an extra hand. You'll be able to see a part of our earth."

Seth put his hand out to help Bernis up. Raven stacked the breakfast dishes for later, scraping all the leftovers into Tulli's dish. The little dog knew that they were going to the deck, so he bypassed the treats for now to help Seth, Raven and ,even now, Bernis.

As they got to the deck, Seth could hear a hard thumping sound. Sometimes bigger fish got caught in the net. He would always get the fish out and throw it back into the ocean. When they started to pull the nets up, it was not a large fish caught in the netting. It was a man, dressed in the same way Bernis was when they first found him. The man was not the same color as Bernis, this man was very dark brown.

Bernis held his breath, "I know this man. I worked with him in the mines.

Oh, law, they had said he was missing on my last shift. I wonder who has done this? Can we pull him up on deck?"

They pulled the dead man out of the water. Bernis knelt down beside him, turning him over as he spoke healing words to himself.

"Look at what is written on his chest! It looks like someone carved it into the very muscle!" Raven held onto her brother as they looked at the man. Someone had written, "So be it with you," across his chest. Everyone stared in horror at the sight.

Bernis wept copious tears. Little Tulli put his body on the man's knees. Imploringly, he looked up to his new friend, trying, in his doggie ways, to see if there was anything he could do. Bernis picked Tulli up cradling him in his heavily muscled arms. The tenderness of this sight got to Raven. She kneeled beside the man, stroking her dog's head, trying to find some way she could help as well.

"Oh law, they will be after me next. After me they will take care of the both of you, even little Tulli. I have to find some way to go back, so you all will be safe."

Bernis handed Tulli to Raven as he stood up. He picked his friend up, taking him to the rails of the boat. He turned to Seth, who motioned that he was OK with what he was about to do. In one fast swoop, he threw his friend clear of the boat, so they could take up the rest of the nets.

"By the law that governs us, my friend Phillip. I send you into the hands of mother ocean. Please take his body to rest, oh mother. He was a good man in word and deed."

Still crying, he turned to help Raven and Seth take up the nets, depositing the fish into the frozen box, so that they would stay fresh until they reached port.

When this was done, Bernis sat upon a thick coil of rope, trying to get ahold of himself.

"Raven, take Tulli down to your quarters, so you can clear up the breakfast mess. Bernis and I must speak to one another, to see what must be done about all of this," Seth said and walked to where the man was, while his sister took her dog down to her quarters.

Bernis began to speak as soon as Raven closed the door, leaving him and Seth alone on the upper deck.

"This man, Phillip, was my friend. We would talk while we were given a time to rest or eat. His crime for incarceration was that he had stole some pies and cakes from the state bakery, run by the Waddis. You see, Phillip and I were from the same earth, but different people. As I was from the Nathas nation, he was from the Theral nation, on the southern half of our planet, where it was warm, with lush rain forests that ranged from one perimeter of their land to the other perimeter. The Waddis were trying to starve the Therals, because the land they lived on was rich in resources. The Therals tried to defend their nation, but the Waddis were too strong. They moved all surviving Therals to small camps, designed to not let them group and overcome the Waddis.

Phillip's family was so hungry that his little daughter fell into a sleep, not wanting to wake up unless she could eat. This six year old child was ready to die! To put herself where pain and starving did not exist. As a father, my friend had to do something. He knew of a bakery where they would throw away in a giant pit, everything that did not sell that day. Of course, this was only for the Waddis. The Therals did not have money to buy anything. Not even jobs to make money were not allowed to them.

So, he went to the pit where all the bakery goods were tossed. Looking all around he did not see anyone. Taking out a bag he had, he began to put anything he could into it. When it was filled, he went through a back way to his house. What he did not know, was that someone had seen him do what he did. As soon as he got to his house, coming in through the back door, there were Waddis already there.

Chapter Two

They took him, and his bag with them. As he looked back, he saw his daughter turn her face to the wall to die. Soon after that he was told that she had died along side her mother. They were buried in a pauper's pit, along with others that had committed similar "crimes."

Seth, I can not leave you and Raven to the Waddis. Law know what they would do to you. I have to rejoin the chain, if I can, tonight. Otherwise I will jump into the ocean to join Phillip," Bernis said as he moved off of the coil of rope, and began pacing the deck.

Seth thought for a moment.
"Bernis, why was making a sentient being so unlawful? I am sure that there are scientists here that experiment on the very same thing. Did you succeed in your experiment?"

Bernis walked up to Seth, hoping he was not invading his space as he did Raven's when they were below deck.

His sky blue eyes twinkled with the amazement he had while doing the experiment.

"Yes, I did succeed, my friend. I made a man, much the same as you and I. Even though he was quite mechanical, he could think and act as a human being. I read books to him, taught him how to read and write, asked him questions to see what his answers were. I was doing all of this in the small house I lived in on the campus of a university where I had to teach Waddis students biology. The parts and machines that I used to make, Adam, as I called him, were all purchased on my own. Some of the machines I made myself. Somehow the Waddis found out about what I was doing. They went to my house when I was not there. I was always careful to put Adam in a little room I had in the back, with lots of books to read. He had no need to eat or drink. Someone within the Waddis that came could imitate my voice. When this person called out, Adam thought it was me and opened the door. I got to my house just as they were finishing him off, grinding what was left of him with their boots, into the hard floor. He was like a child to me! How could they do that? I made him as a companion, a friend. They annihilated him! They arrested me right there on the spot. Without trial, I was sent to the mines." Bernis said and hung his head down.

Seth knew that Raven would never forgive him if he let Bernis do what he wanted to do. There had to be a way to end this thing, not only helping this man, but all the others that were sentenced by the Waddis for a crime that was only in their corrupt, mean spirited ways. Oh, but what to do! He put his hands on Bernis' wide shoulders, and in the smallest breath he could take he whispered so no one else could hear,

"My sister and I will help you and all

As both men watched the sails fill with air. Bernis was amazed at how tranquil it made him feel. What he did not fathom was an underwater shape, not like any fish you would ever see. It was following every move the boat would make. If only he had noticed the movement, perhaps Seth and himself could figure it out. For now it remained a shadow, riding on the current in the deep water.

Raven walked out to the deck after finishing her chores in the boat's kitchen. She put Tulli down. The little dog ran swiftly into Bernis waiting arms. He heartily licked his face, letting him smell all the left overs the dog had just eaten.

He hugged the little dog closely to his chest, smelling his little doggie smell, enjoying the constant licking of his face. He did not want to forget this dog, these people. The large shadow passed beneath the boat, riding in its wake. Stealthy it was as it glided unseen within the waters beneath.

Seth shouted as they neared the shore. The people that bought his fish would be waiting for him. Tulli turned in Bernis' arms, wanting to look ahead. The little dog sensed something that was going along with them. Lacking language skills, he would yip, and sneeze,trying to let the man know that something was stalking them. Rachel walked over to take the little dog. To her astonishment he growled at her. She knew then and there that Tulli had sensed something was amiss, working with the dog as she did gave her the knowledge to gauge his signs.

He was not growling at her, he was telling her something was wrong, and it had to do with the man. Immediately she told Bernis of this, telling him to be on his guard. Raven motioned to her brother, telling him what was suspect. They were too close to shore to stop, so it was to be handled when they landed. He gathered Bernis, who was still holding Tulli, and took Raven's hand. As they saw their friends on land, these people knew something was going on. They had made an agreement some years before that if ever there was any trouble, he would stand with his sister and anyone else who was with them, on the deck of the boat. Their friends immediately sent a boat out with two men in it, to bring everyone to port, fish and all, without touching the water. The danger was still beneath them, waiting.

For what it was, there was all the time anything had to offer. It wasn't going anywhere.

Fish, Raven, Seth, Tulli, and Bernis all made it to land safely. As they went ashore, Bernis turned around to look at the boat. That was when he saw it. There was an enveloping darkness under the boat. He pointed it out to Seth and Raven, while Tulli, trembling, clung to Bernis' chest.

"As soon as we are done with the exchange of the fish, we will go see that friend I spoke about. My friends here will watch the boat and take care of anything else while we are gone."

The two elders that stood behind gave their affirmation to Seth, as well as the men who had helped them from the boat to the shore. Where they were these things had been here before. This island was one of a chain of islands that had the very mystery of life ingrained within their core. You had to be careful here, physically and spiritually.

The elder man spoke to the woman he was with," Evangeline, we must be very careful of this one. I believe the blackness under the boat is a dimensional rift, or hole. If we are not careful, all of us will be in danger. I hope that Seth is going to see Thomasina. I think she might be the only one capable of doing anything, as far as this is concerned."

The elder man put his hand on the shoulder of the woman. She could not keep her eyes off of the enveloping blackness that was under the boat.

"Father Damien, this rift is so that it can only harm living things, not boats or wood. Even the fish of the ocean avoid it. Look how they are swimming far around the boat, rather than close, as they always do. You are right, though, we must be very careful in how we handle this. Seth has not experienced anything like this before. Thomasina needs to come to the shore, so she can see the whole picture.

Only that way she will be able to solve this puzzle. I am afraid, Father," She said and gripped Father Damien's hand so hard, it hurt the old man's arthritis. He did not mumble any protest. He was too busy looking at the danger beneath the boat.

Seth led the way to Thomasina's house. Tulli had relaxed quite a bit since they had left the boat, then the shore. He was pleasantly sleeping in Bernis' strong arms. The man would not let go of the little dog. He kept him calm as they were walking. Raven saw that,keeping her wish to hold her little dog to herself. She had used Tulli in much the same way, when her and her brother would get into some troubles while fishing in the deep ocean. She was glad to be on land, and to smell the wonderful flowers that grew on this island.

"Thomasina's house should be another two miles this way.

We will have to climb a little, as she lives on the side of the great mountain here," Seth said as he pointed out the cloud capped mountain before them. About half way up was a little house. It was tiny to some, but just perfect to Thomasina.

She also had a small garden on the backside of the house. Raven pointed its location to Bernis, still cuddling little Tulli.

"Do not worry, my lady. I have climbed, walked, ran, everything one would do when mining in the peaks of Challaque. The mines were half way up the peaks. We also had to carry all the slag down the peaks. The people that live there only rented the area to the Wallis. I think that they might have been afraid most the indigenous people there. They are very tall and strong because of where they live on their earth. It is not easy to live on the third earth. Even though I was a convict I was glad to leave there when we were done for the day. The conditions there were far worse than where we lived," Bernis said and petted Tulli softly as to not awaken him. This small gesture helped him cope with what they had to do. He already loved the little dog. Raven could see that well.

They began their last turn on the path to Thomasina's house. She had already seen them from far away, even as they left the boat to yet another boat to get them safely to shore. She knew of the monster that lurked beneath the boat. Neither natural or mechanical this beast that had hinged itself to travel with the boat. She could feel the manipulation of it from a far star dimension, that was certainly not something to take lightly. It had all to do with the extra man travelling with them.

"Hello, my beloveds! It has been a while since I have seen you last. Come let me hug you, and give you both the kisses you deserve. I see you have one more. Tulli has taken to this one, that is a good sign. Any times an animal takes to you, they bond their spirit to yours. No matter where you are, apart or not, they will be your protector. Here, let me hug you. You look like you might need one," Thomasina said and had to reach on her tippy toes, as she was rather small in regards to Bernis' bulk. Tulli gave her a kiss as she hugged the man.

"My lady, I am honored to meet you. You must be very brave to live all the way up here, alone. I hope you get help when you need it. My name is Bernis. I can not believe how quiet and beautiful it is up here. The whole island smells like my mother's flower garden in my home earth. It brings me so much pleasure to remember her. She has been gone for many years," Bernis recounted and began to stroke Tulli's head as he spoke. The dog did not mind it at all. He loved the man, after all.

What Bernis did not know, was that Thomasina was Raven's and Seth's aunt. She was their father's only sibling, his sister. This lady was no one to be messed with. Beyond her cognitive powers, lay her capability to cure sickness, read palms, see the future, this list goes on and on. That is why she lived alone, except for a very large goose named Titan. If he hadn't been locked in his stall, he would have been all over Bernis, the only one he did not know. Everyone knew of his presence because of his persistent and loud honking. Finally, she excused herself for a moment, taking Bernis in tow.

"I have to have you meet Titan. Otherwise, he would have your ears bitten to bits! Come, here we go, around this corner." Thomasina took a small key out of her pocket. Titan was honking even louder, now that he knew his mistress was near. Slowly,she opened the door to his stall, which was quite large, due to the fact of how large this goose really was. He could actually look into Bernis' eyes with no problem.

Bernis waited a little behind Thomasina, as to not upset the goose. He was stroking Tulli's head very slowly while looking in awe at this enormous goose. When the door was finally opened, the goose stopped honking,staring at the stranger. Intently, he waddled over to Bernis, who smiled, a little nervously, at Titan. As the goose got closer he sighted Tulli in the man's arms, looking very content to be where he was. That was good enough for him. He stretched his wings out, taking the man, the dog and Thomasina in a very big hug. Thomasina managed to wiggle out a little bit, she could not get her breath in the middle of all these creatures.

"Looks like you have made a new friend. Titan does not do this to everyone. You must be a very special person. You should be proud of yourself."

The goose gradually loosened his grip, allowing one and all to get some air. As they all turned to go back where Seth and Raven were, Titan took flight with a great whoosh. He landed spot on, several feet away from the startled brother and sister. Raven was taken aback by all that was going on. She knew Bernis was a good person. She also knew that the threat under the boat was following this same man. Their lives were all in danger. Then here was this ginormous goose acting like a little child, dancing with delight in front of everyone. Bernis stood by her. As he did, he softly handed Tulli over to his mistress.

"You have a grand little dog here, Lady. He makes me feel human again. You take him for a while, so we can figure out what to do about this predicament. I know that I have put you all in great danger. With Thomasina's help, I hope to rid you all and myself of this terror. The best thing would be to free all my people on earth then. If we could, you would be considered as a hero in the stars by everyone on my earth. Let us hope that, at least, we can save ourselves, and my precious Tulli," As soon as Bernis said the dog's name, he jumped from Raven's arms to his. This, indeed, made a tear flow from both of their eyes.

Thomasina knew the scene playing before them well. Her parents had fled their earth of origin. They were vast sweeps of populations that were exterminated on their home earth because of the color of their skin, central beliefs, religions, and most of all, their language. Her parents spoke the indigenous language of their ancestors, Shemish. They knew that the time had come for them to run. And that they did to this ninth earth. It seemed peaceful enough, then.

Things were beginning to change. She could see the horizon changing all around her. That's why she lived here, alone, on this tiny speck of island called Turmond, after the man who had found it so many years before. Many of the things she thought about and witnessed, she never told Seth and Raven. Maybe it was time to do it. For now, she would feed her guests.

"Come my favorite and only niece and nephew. I am going to fix you a feast of my newly harvested vegetables, along with a cheese like no other. Turmond had the best cheddar that anywhere else."

Raven's eyes perked up when she heard her aunt speak about the cheese. She hadn't had any cheese in months. She quickly volunteered to help her aunt. Titan followed them as they went into her cottage.

The goose knew his place in Thomasina's house.

He had a large round pillow that he would sit on. He knew that if he did not,there would be no tasty treats coming from the kitchen. He murmured a waddling noise to himself as he sat there in his favorite spot, hoping he would get some of that tasty cheese. Bernis and Seth walked into the house, making sure to brush the bottom of their shoes. It was a tradition always transacted at anyone's door, to make sure no "road dirt" made it into the inner sanctum of the house. They were already smelling the delicious odors wafting their way from the kitchen to their noses. Both of them found a spot to sit,allowing room for Titan, on the large pillow where he was. He floated one giant wing halfway in the air, then swept it across the empty spaces on either side of the pillow. Both men knew where they were supposed to sit.

Thomasina was cooking a big vegetable goulash, flavored with the many spices she grew in her mountain garden. Raven was focused on getting correct, thin slices of the large wheel of Turmond cheddar cheese. The aunt looked at her only niece, remarking to herself how much she looked like her mother. The same black as midnight hair,hanging well past her waist. Her liquid black eyes, scrunching up as she carefully sliced each piece of cheese. It made her eyes steam up as they do when she ever thought of family. No tears, just a searing hotness in each eye, making it difficult to focus. Yes, before anything else, she would have to tell them of what happened so many years before. What made her father so solemn, and watchful.

Yes, yes, after the eating then the explaining would begin. Many plates full of delicious treats made their way to the living room table. Goulash, cheese, all kinds of raw vegetables sliced so they could be dipped into the dressing Thomasina had made. Crusty slices of homemade bread, spread with yellow butter, just waiting to be devoured. Titan was being a good goose,sitting there between Seth and Bernis. As they got their plates filled, Raven filled a plate for Tulli and Titan. Each impatiently waited for their food, tapping their feet. Titan was getting louder with his "waddling."

Soon everyone had their plates. Thomasina bent her head in benediction, just as Tulli and Titan did. Seth, Raven, and Bernis followed example, bowing their heads as well.

"Thank you earth for giving us this wonderful lunch. Thank you God of good for all of my visitors. Oh yes, let us not forget our beloved companions Titan and Tulli. Thank you for our blessings. Amen."

Everyone tucked into the repast, washing it down with cold, clear water from the mountain. While they ate, Thomasina thought of everything she had to tell her beloved niece and nephew.

What was sad was that there could have been more, so many years ago. The grief welled up in her throat, causing her to cough. She passed it off as bread being stuck in her throat.

Seth and Bernis offered to clean up after their meal. Titan had fallen into a pleasant nap on his pillow, nesting his head under his rather large wing. What Thomasina called "waddling," emanated from under his wing. Thomasina's eyes glistened with small tears, peeking out of the ends of each eye. Raven felt something was wrong with her aunt.

"Auntie Tom, are you alright? There seems to be something going on in your mind. Would you like to share?" The girl said and put her warm hands against her aunt's work worn hands. Tulli had fallen to sleep by her side, his tummy full of all the treats his mistress and the man fed him.

"My sweet girl, there are many things we must discuss. I would like to speak about some things when Seth comes back. Bernis is welcome to listen. I know in my heart of hearts that he is a good man. He has been through much the same as your father and I did. parents suffered even more than any of us did. Can you go and see if the coffee is ready yet? I will sit here so I can compose my thoughts."

Thomasina gained the lap Tulli wanted to sleep on, allowing her to meditate on the facts before the children came back. Raven went into the kitchen to see if the coffee was ready yet. As she approached the door, she could see her brother and Bernis finishing the clean up. The little pot of coffee was singing on the top of the stove. She removed the pot because Thomasina had an ancient wood stove that she had found on the mountain when she first moved here, so many years before. Seth helped to get the cups, milk, and sugar for the tray, while Bernis finished putting away everything they cleaned. The kitchen sparkled with fellowship. She could tell that the man had much on his mind,so when she went over to let him know what they were doing, she did it slowly, deliberately. Seth carried the tray of cups, sugar, and milk. Bernis followed with the coffee pot. Raven came in last with a neatly sliced tray of small tea cakes she had brought with her. She knew that her aunt loved these little pastries that could only be found on the mainland of Tarsis. They had sold their last fish trawl there, and had gotten top dollar for their work.

"Oh, you remembered the cakes. It has been a while since I have had anything sweet, except for fruit from my trees, of course."

Thomasina's face lit up like a bright ray of sunshine on a gloomy day.

She appreciated all that "her kids" did for her. After their father and mother died, she was the last connection to the past.

"It must be said right now," she whispered to herself.

"As we are all sitting here, full of good food. Now we are going to finish our meal with coffee and my favorite tea cakes. There is something that I must be truthful about to you Seth, and you, Raven. Bernis, you are welcome to stay here and listen to what I am going to say. It might even remind you of something," She said and looked at all of them, one at a time to make her point.

"I hope that all of you will understand that what I am about to say is very important. It may have happened in the past, but it has all to do with the future. We are supposed to learn from our pasts. Sometimes there are those of us that do not. Those that refrain from the prior knowledge are often doomed to repeat it. So, here it goes, my loves. Raven, please make me a cup of that divine coffee. You know how I like it, love."

Thomasina patted Raven's hand as she reached to get the coffee pot. She smiled at her aunt, wondering why with all that was going on, she decided to do this. Who knew? It might help them in what they are trying to accomplish. Bernis handed her the sugar bowl, touching her hand as he did. The man's hand was warm, workworn, and imparted a bit of the person in him. She felt a surge of pure kindness. Her eyes rose to meet his. Both knew that there was thank you within the unspoken silence.

"I have to tell you about your father's and my parents, Opesh and Malil. They were born on earth two. Each one was a member of the Schmeshina nation.

Their native language was Shemish. On the earth that they lived on, a strange people came there from another dimension, through the wormhole that threads itself between the earths. Few know how it works to go from earth to earth, but these people did. This band of hooligans was called the Waddis. They were mean, heartless, and only wanted the peaceful nations of earth two to serve them as laborers. Where they labored was up to them, but it was hard, backbreaking work. The Waddis had no soul, no goodness, not a kindness ever crossed their thin, skeletal lips," Thomasina stopped because of a guttural noise she heard coming from Bernis. It was almost like he was choking.

"I am sorry to interrupt your story, my lady. It was the Waddis who captured my nation as well. I do not know what to say," Bernis said as he held his head in his hands, trying to get ahold of himself.

Titan woke up with the commotion, instantly knowing what was going on. With one gentle swoop of his wing, he took Bernis into a grasp so he could calm him down. Within a few minutes, he began to get ahold of the situation. All this time, Titan was speaking in a low waddling tone, that soothed the man beside him.

" I am so sorry that I dredged up this memory from you, Bernis. I had no idea that the Waddis was associated with your being on a chain gang, so to speak. My story will interest you more, my new friend. Because through the story I tell of a way to escape these villians. I must keep it going for the sake of Seth and Raven. They must know the whole story from beginning to end, before I can not tell it any more. Now, let us take up where I left off," Thomasina said and took a long sip from her cup, settling herself in her pillow chair.

All on the island of Turmond sat on pillows or pillow chairs. No real chairs were ever used in this island nation. Tables were only used to prepare food. When people sat down to eat, they sat on their pillows on the floor, stretched a large cloth between them. Setting all their food upon this easy way of having any meal.

Thomasina cleared her throat, getting ready to speak again, "I promise what ever I will tell to you all, is the truth. I will try and not take too long, for there are monsters to breech. Yes, the Waddis invaded earth two from their infernal dimension. Opesh and Malil were put in the same work camp, but different houses. We children, your father, Marcus, myself, and our two brothers; Thesus and Mishem stayed with our mother, Malil. It was very hard to bear, being away from our father. We were all so close to each other. Thesus and Mishem were just little boys at the time.

They were quite miserable, because they had to work as hard as our mother did, as we all did. We never got enough to eat, so we slowly started to starve to death. It was then that our mother and father somehow got ahold of one another through the camp underground network. They decided there was nothing to loose;the parley was made that we all would meet up in the dark woods behind the camp. Mama had told all of us to be very quiet, so we would not be discovered. A sick and dying man took our father's place in his bed, so, if anything was discovered, the Waddis would look for the wrong man. Where we lived, the women of the house, put their own sick babies in our beds. There was a nursing mother who was very sick with the pocks. Her baby had it too, and would not live long. She took her place in Mama's bed. So sad, so very sad. It had to be done in order for some of us to survive.

Two other families went with us. Their
trail was also disguised as ours. Everyone
hoped that some of us would survive. We
all knew that not everyone would make
it. Papa had to carry Mishem, he was very
frail, and so tired. He did not mind
carrying the boy. Thesus was about ten
years old then, so he could keep up with
Marcus and I. We were all headed for a
rendezvous within the dark forest, where
there was supposed to be a fragment of
an old worm hole that would take those
who used it to different earths. There was
no choice of which earth to go to. You just
went where ever the worm hole sent you.
As we approached the fragment, there
were two men standing there, holding it
open for us. They had also risked their
lives to be there. Everyone was tense as
we approached the fragment. Papa
decided that we would go first, so we all
stood, tightly bunched together within
the fragment. We were told not to let go
of any of our group, so we all held hands

as best we could. The wormhole sucked us up within its web. As we were travelling through it, the wormhole somehow passed high over the camp. All was dark and tired, no one could be seen. We were all so busy hanging on to one another that we did not notice that Mishem had died as soon as he came into contact with the worm hole. Thesus held tightly to Marcus, Mama, Papa and I, squeezing my eyes tightly, not wanting to see anything else until we landed. Within minutes we came to this earth, number nine. But, all was not well. Thesus had landed upon a boulder, cracking his skull. He was gone in seconds. It was then we discovered that Mishem was dead. Mama fell to the ground covered with grief, not making a sound. We did not know where we had landed yet, which we would find out later would be the ninth earth. Papa and Marcus buried the little ones as deep as they could. They did not want any wild animals to take them.

Mama's silent tears fell to the earth beneath her feet. Mama and Papa were heartbroken, but they had to save their remaining children even as they grieved. It was good luck to end up on earth nine. Papa and Marcus set to building the house you see here around us. Mama and I started a small garden from seeds that we were given by the people who found us. They also gave us this side of the mountain. Although the mountain has its own name, which is Piedmont, after the peppers that grow wild here. Papa named our little patch of land, Mishem-Thesus, after my little brothers. Their grave is just beyond the little rise at the back of the garden. Papa had asked the people that owned this side of the mountain if he could rent the land from them. They knew the story of how the boys had died, burying them near a large ancient cairn. This island, despite its remoteness has seen its share of the trudging of different feet.

The owners were Mayvis and Martin. They were quite elderly, raising their only grandchild, Ravenna. Ah yes, my little bird, your mother. Their family had lived and owned the while mountain for many generations. They had divided the mountain into four sections, three of whom were given to their three surviving children. Ravenna the daughter of their youngest son, had been orphaned since she was a wee baby. She did not want the land for herself, but for the family they had saved and brought her future husband, Marcus. As soon as those two set eyes on one another, it was all over. We had been lucky in some ways that others did not get. Before Papa died he had heard from an old friend of his that had escaped from the Waddis and earth two. He told us that the Waddis had caught one of the families that were trying to go through the fragment. They killed the children first, before their parents, then slowly strangled the parents while their children died in front of them. This friend of his had been one of the men holding the fragment open for the families to travel through it. His brother had been there helping him. As soon as the Waddis got ahold of his brother, he pushed Seth through the fragment to freedom. Yes, my love, that is where your name came from. Your grandfather had asked your father, Marcus, to name his firstborn son after his friend and rescuer. It meant a lot to Papa. After Papa died, Mama wanted to cremate him, as they had done for generations in the nation of Shemishina. She kept him in a little ornate box that he had made for her when we first landed on this earth. Sadly enough, we did not bring anything with us from the second earth. Anything our father made for her, she cherished. Several years before Mama died, she would sit me down after dinner, telling me all of the ancient stories. My memory has always been a hurt point for me.

I wrote everything Mama told me into this book," Thomasina said as she took out a large book, covered in parchment. After showing it, she put it down in front of her. Everyone's eyes were focused on that book. Each one wondered what treasures might be found within its pages.

"Well, this ramble must be finished, so we can help Bernis. I will let you all read it tonight after dinner. For now, let me finish with Mama and Marcus. Mama died thirty years after Papa. Her skin was so translucent you could see her veins working the blood in her body. Marcus and Ravenna had taken over the fishing boat from her grandparents. They still lived here, but they had to fish for weeks at a time to provide for all of us. I decided to stay here with Mama until she died. Then Marcus and Ravenna learned she was pregnant with Seth. Marcus would do the fishing, and leave Ravenna with me.

When Mama died, even though she was
pregnant, she helped me to cremate her.
After that was over, we spaded up all her
ashes, putting them in the same box with
my father. She wanted it that way. Then
we buried them in the same cairn with
Thesus and little Mishem. You may go
and see the cairn after a while. Let us take
a small break, then we will get to saving
Bernis and his planet, if we can,"
Thomasina finished and put her cup
down. Within seconds she was asleep,
softly snoring in her chair.

Chapter Three

Titan had his head under his wing, making soft waggle noises as he slept. Seth, Raven and Bernis went outside to get some air, clear their heads a little. The sun had not reached midday yet. The morning shadows were still promoting their magic on the side of the mountain. Tulli had decided to take the time to roll in the dewy grass, growling as he did. The beauty of the Piedmont rested their souls, allowing them to clearly think over what had to be done.

"Seth, Bernis; let us go and pay our respects to our grandparents and uncles. Mom and Dad aren't there yet. We have to wait until the first full moon of the year. That is when we will bring them home," mists of tears blinded Raven and she stumbled upon a rock, falling to the ground. Bernis was quick to her side, checking to see if she was injured in any way.

"I am all right my friend. The only

thing I hurt was my fragile ego," Raven said as she leaned on the rock she stumbled over. her weight was not much, but she could feel the rock turning beneath her hand. Startled, she turned to see what was controlling it. As she was looking at the rock, Seth was rendered speechless at the sight he beheld. The cairn, the old tomb; there was a slab that covered it. When Raven stumbled over the rock, she must have triggered something.

"Hey, look at this! That was no rock sister. That thing you fell over is a mechanism to open the cairn. Our grandparents and uncles burials underscored the cairn, making it next to impossible to open. Look, under the rock, Raven. Is there not a metal grasper there?" Seth shouted and was jumping up and down as she checked under the rock. To be sure there was a hard metal grasper there, unrusted after leaving it in the soil for perhaps centuries.

"What shall we do? Raven quavered.

"We should see if Thomasina has some candles, torches, or even a lantern. Seth, stay where you are, I will go and get your aunt. Raven, are you OK, my lady?" Bernis said and turned his head as he sprinted to the cabin, seeing that Raven affirmed that all was right.

But, as Bernis was going to seek Thomasina, she was already there, "I knew there was something there. I just never could find it. With all my know how, I never located the right place. I had always known there was a door there. Never figured how it could open. Here is a lantern for each of you. Do not separate, keep together in this first look at what lies beneath," She handed the lamps to Bernis, and he kissed her on the cheek, making her blush bright red. Titan stood right beside her, with one large wing around her for protection.

"Titan, I know who you really are, as you know in me the same. For all my capabilities, I never figured out about the cairn opening in such a way. Do you remember when I tried to get you to move the stone? With all your strength, it didn't move an inch. One thing for sure, Bernis is the man for Raven. I will let them figure it out on their own. I hope they survive all of this to be able to discover what each of them is worth. I think I will sit here, under this old apple tree, eat a bit of fruit, drink some cool water, and wait for them to come out of the cairn. Would you like to join me Titan?" Thomasina asked and put her hand on the goose' head. He started to waggle softly in her ear. She knew what it meant, as he sat beside his mistress.

Inside the cairn was damp and cold. As they went further down, with lanterns lit, the steam that came off of the little lights within. Their breaths staged a dance with the steam, undulating around each other's energy in a straggled chorus. Raven had an old shirt tied around her waist. She had always done this because, with Seth, you never know what you would get into, and would have to help out. She gave the shirt to Bernis to wear, because he had no shirt on. She could see his muscles quiver in the dim light. She buttoned it up for him, because she was not sure that he knew what buttons were. The man laughed under his breath. He felt like he was a child again, his mother buttoning his shirt for him. He always forgot to button, because he was always in a hurry to get things done so he could go to school. She would always sing to him as she buttoned him up. How he missed his mother, delicate, yet strong in her beliefs.

"Hey you two, let's get a move on. The mid day has almost come. Let's see what this cairn tunnel has, we might be able to use something from here. You never know what might be found in something like this!" Seth shouted as he quickly walked towards a strange lump in not far from them. Bending down, he could make out characters dug into the surface of the rock. Once the rock had been smooth on that side. Years and moisture had caused mold to grow over the inscriptions. Near his knee, in the dirt,he saw what looked like a brush. When he picked it up, he could see that this was no brush. It was the skeletal remains of a small animal's tail. The vertebrae had little branch looking bone, that once held the creature's tail in check. He used this to brush off the inscriptions. Just as he was finishing, Bernis kneeled beside him.

"I know this script. It is a common script used by the Waddis! I can read it, if you will let me," Bernis said and got as close as he could with his lantern. The closer he got, the more he realised the importance of what was written.

"OK, here it goes. It says that the Waddis came here in the year of the dog. They stayed here for a while but could not find any human to do their work. Trying to make an established colony here was impossible. There was only a slight fragment left on this mountain. It would be many years before there would be anything that could be used for travelling between earths and dimensions. This individual might have been the last one of his company. In the tail of the inscription, he says to go to the vaulted room in the middle of the cairn. The company there had scribed a stellar map, telling where all the fragments and worm holes that they knew about," Bernis continued and was scratching his head, because the whole thing was amazing and incredulous. It baffled him that this particular Waddis wrote like a human.

"Let's go around this way to see what we can find," Seth said as he got off of the dirt. As he was first, he was also the one to see what was there first. All Raven and Bernis could hear was his shrill whistle, echoing off of the walls of the cairn. They hurried their steps to get where he was. When Bernis and Raven came to where Seth was, they could hardly believe their eyes. In front of them was a huge stellar map. It told where the twenty earths were located throughout the galaxies. Tied to each earth was a wormhole, sometimes two or three. There were also fragments the Waddis had found throughout the surrounding solar systems. It even located the fragment that they tried to use on the mountainside. There was one thing that astounded them all. Below all the earths there was a portal inscribed. It was depicted round and circular, bending continuously, turning in on itself. There was a very large wormhole coming from the dimension, and looping itself to, at least, five of the earths.

Each earth was numbered, so they could
tell where they were going and how. The
most astonishing thing was a mound
directly under the inscription. On top of
the mound was a single skeleton. The
long fingerbones, elongated skull, large
eyesockets with a small brow ridge over
them, and five long toes of equal length
on each foot told who this "person"had
been. This had been a Waddis of the
highest order. There was a baton, topped
with a strange looking mammal, still
hanging on to the remains of the left
hand. Bernis picked up the baton, curious
to see if he could recognise the animal on
the top. Cleaning off the grime and dirt
from it, the animal recognition came to a
peak.

"Ho! I know this animal. The
Waddis used to raise them and use them
to hunt humans. It may look small, but its
mouth was large, and it has thorn like
protrusions on its tail. To us, it was
deadly, because the barbs on its tail

contained flesh eating poison. One of these get ahold of you, that would be it. I may be wrong, but I believe they call them "Utrus", which is Waddis for eat. This thing gives me chills," Bernis exclaimed and threw the baton on the ground. Tulli tried to smell it, but whimpered away from it, running to Bernis to pick him up.

Raven was very curious about the mound that the skeleton was laying on. When she looked at the pelvis, it shocked her to the very core of her being. Every time she had heard of the Waddis, they were always referred to as a he. This skeleton, somewhat anthropomorphic, was definitely a female! She saw the bones of the pelvis, upturned as they were, notches and scratches where the opening would be. This particular Waddis had birthed at least two children. She had studied anatomy when she was at school, long before her parents passed away.

The first skeleton that she saw was not a human skeleton, but a Waddis skeleton that had been found in a cave many years before. She remembered the pelvis looked just like this one. It made her more determined to see what lay in the mound underneath. Bernis and Seth were busy taking notes on the star map, so, while their attention was elsewhere, she dug into the side of the mound, about floor level. She hoped to find an answer to this mystery.

As Raven was digging through the side of the mound, she was not aware of what was happening around her. It was almost like she had ventured into another world. Bernis was busy deciphering the script on the star map. Seth was equally busy trying to keep up with what he was being told. No one noticed that the baton had rolled, by itself, over to a close corner. The filial had popped off of the baton, exposing rolled up paper that had been secreted within the hollow.

Seth stepped back a few paces to get a better look at the map, while Bernis was trying to read what was inscribed on the top of the map. He was now rolling a boulder towards the map so he could read the rest of the script on top. All this was happening around the vault within the cairn. Seth began to slide, then fall, because he had stepped on something round. While he sat there on the floor,he noticed the baton. Curiosity got the best of him. Before Bernis could make it to pick him up, he had picked up the baton. Seth handed Bernis the baton when he freely stood up. Raven was still digging under the mound. She held forth her lantern, to be able to see within the grave. In the dimness of the light and swirling dirt, she saw an ornate box in front of her. It was quite wide and a bit long from what she could tell. Turning around to go out of the mound, she crawled to the opening. She could see Seth and Bernis looking at some papers.

Perhaps someone could help her.

"Hey, can one of you guys help me here? I think that I have found something very important," Raven was waiving her arms with the excitement of the find. Seth left Bernis to the papers,going to help his sister.

"OK, sis. Let us see what is here." Seth crawled halfway into the tunnel Raven had carved into the mound. Slowly he held his lantern up, not really realising what he was up against. He looked carefully at the box, taking the lantern all around it. Besides where his sister had dug, there was a dome like opening around the box. To him it looked important enough. The handle on the small end looked in good shape. He tested it by pulling a little. The handle stayed put, so he put a little more hand strength onto it, and pulled it again. This time it slid towards him. Slowly he pulled on it until he could see his sister's lantern at the entrance of the tunnel.

"I am scared, Seth. What if it contains some horrible disease? We could all be gone in a minute," Raven said and held herself together by putting her arms around her waist. Every nerve in her body was on fire.

Bernis walked over to the opening and said, "I do not think that it is something to worry about,except as far as ancient history is concerned," holding the papers in his hands, he stood there, beside Raven, until Seth cleared the tunnel. The box was half in and half out of the hole. It seemed as if it was there, waiting for them to discover its contents.

The Letter;

To those of you who are reading this missive, welcome. What ever is said by these words are about those of us who are long gone. There might be some descendants still alive on this earth.

If they are,please give them this, so they can read my story and learn from it. My name is Martiz, high princess of the Urtrus baton. This name means little to me now, as I have just buried, beneath the mound, my beloved Kem, our baby girl Misha, and our son Thomas, aged only ten years. Oh, my heart is broken, along with most of my bones. I know, as a half Waddis, my bones can still knit themselves new. Unfortunately, my sweet children were only one fourth Waddis, my beautiful husband was human. They died within a rock fall, of which I was buried in as well. Somehow I managed to drag myself out, as I tried to save my family. I can still hear little Misha's cries in my heart as I write this. When I got all of them out the children were already gone. My beautiful, sweet husband managed to live a few hours before he died in my arms. I feel so useless!There is one thing though. Not long ago, I sent my oldest son to live with his human grandparents. They desperately needed his help in their little farm on the side of the Piedmont.

His name is Tennif, after his Waddis grandfather. The grandparent's given name is Pond. I hope that it fares well with them. They seemed like good people, and they were Kem's parents. I am sorry, reader. My tears are messing up the papers. I was fortunate to have an oblong box, that we had used to bring the tools into the cairn. I have already decorated it for my little family. As I put each one of them in, making sure that they fit right. I also domed my shield with its boss facing up, over them, protective. That is how we bury loved ones in our parallel dimension. There is really no name for that place, as inhospitable as it is. It will always be referred to as "home world."

I put the earth over my loves in a dome shape, with my shield protecting them forever. If you do take them out, please put my remains along with my husband and children. Then just put us under the shield, and all will be well. I just want to say that not all Waddis are the horrid things humans take us for.

My mother was human, and my father Waddis. It is not common, but accepted, if a Waddis man prefers a human partner to a Waddis partner. My mother was a very loving, sweet human. She loved my father with all her heart. He was always afraid that he would die before her. That did not happen. Mama died with the flux after her and Papa had been together for twenty years. How he mourned her passing. How we all mourned her death.

Dear reader, I digress. Please take advantage of the star map. It catalogues all the wormholes and fragments correctly. You can also see home world portal below. This earth has been my true home world for some years now. I was left behind while the other Waddis took the wormhole out, destroying it into fragments as they left.

Kem and his parents found me, near death on the Piedmont. Even though I was considered a Waddis,this did not bother them. They loved me anyway.

You can not live without love. Bear witness that the Waddis can not take love. It makes them sick. As they shall remain, unloved, and disgusting to the sight. I know that this might astonish you, but you will find that I am right. We built the cairn as a refuge from anything that could come from there. We did not know how long the fragments would take to repair themselves. I only know what is now. Read this, and keep it until you find my son Tennif Pond's descendants. Give it to them for to do what they will with it.

Now, I die as the only way a Waddis can. I rammed my head into the rock wall at the back of the cairn, bumping it hard enough for my skull to crack. Follow the star chart, reader. I hope that I am able to go to human heaven, forgiven of my sins, to be with my beloved Kem, holding my babies in my arms until they ache with the love they bear. I do not know what decade we are in. When I arrived here it was the year of the dog.

By earth terms, it would have been many generations back, when this is read. Goodbye dear reader. I go now.

-Martiz

All at once, the three stared at each other. It took a few minutes for all the story to sink in. Bernis tucked the baton, with the papers within into his belt. The filial scratched a bit, so he wrapped it up with a bit of his shirt, putting it back into his belt. The Urtus would have to eat someone else for lunch. With a learned reverence, he carefully picked up Martiz's skeleton. Waddis did not have ligaments like humans did. They had a tough stringy, fibrous line that kept all the bones together. He felt like he was picking up a child's doll. Seth and Raven opened the makeshift coffin, preparing themselves for the worst. As they opened it they both caught the smell of cut grass and flowers. When they had slowly opened the top to its last point, they could see the figures of a robust man, holding a small baby girl. Beside him was a small boy, with his hands holding his father's leg. They looked so serene, like they were asleep.

Raven began to weep, influenced by the letter, and by what she was seeing. It was almost too much. She grabbed Tulli, holding him close to her.

Bernis took the skeleton, placing it within a hollow on the other side of Kem. As soon as she rested there, he could see her beauty,within and without. He choked back a tear. He did not want to look too attached to the remains of this remarkable woman. But, it was too late. Copious tears soon found their way down his cheeks. Seth seemed to be the only one not touched by this scene. He made sure that all the bodies had their place within the box. There was a small bunch of straw flowers growing within the outside door of the cairn.

He asked Raven to get them for him. When she did, he took them from her placing them carefully on Martiz's body. Bernis helped Seth close the lid, pushing the box back within the mound. When it centered under the shield, a slight gong could be heard, like it was far away. They all made sure that the hole was filled up. Each one of them shuffled their feet over the mound, so no one could tell it had been opened. They picked up all their notes and lanterns. Leaving the cairn as they entered it.

Thomasina was still under the apple tree. She was reading from a little book she held in her hands. Titan was waggling around the yard, looking for bugs to eat. The elder lady looked up from her book, "I was only going to give you one half hour more, then I was going in after you all! Is everyone alright? It is almost lunch time. We can discuss whatever you all saw down there over food. I always eat cold food for lunch.

Don't want to cook for every meal. How does Tormund cheese sandwiches, with lettuce and tomatoes grown on the Piedmont. We can chase it with some sweet apple juice, maybe a boiled chicken egg or two for you big boys. I am sure you are hungry, because you all must have been busy. Just look at the dirt on your clothes! Shake them off before you enter my house please!" She turned her back to them to go to her house.

Bernis took that opportunity to close the latch, thus closing the cairn until next time. He did not want the elder lady to bother with the cairn.

"She might not comprehend what was there," he thought to himself. He surely did not want her to get hurt. So, he took off his shirt, because that was the only bit of clothing he wore besides his breeches. The baton whacked him in the side as he was arranging himself, wondering if Thomasina should even see the papers

within the baton. He would let Seth and Raven decide that. He bent down to scoop up Tulli, and continued to walk towards the tiny house.

Thomasina made the sandwiches in nothing flat. Soon, everyone was stretched out in her front room, Titan sitting on his pillow, with Seth and Bernis on either side. He was too busy eating all the fruit and vegetables Thomasina had cut up for him to eat. Everything settled, the elder lady turned her attention to Raven, who sat right below her right knee.

"What did you find of interest in the cavern, my sweet girl. It must have been something interesting, due to all the dirt that was on your clothes, plus the amount of time you all spent there."

Raven swallowed her bite of sandwich, reaching for her glass of water so she wouldn't choke. She felt very nervous,but only one sentence came out of her mouth,"Aunt, did you ever know of a family with the last name of Pond living here on the Piedmont?"

Thomasina dropped her sandwich on her plate. She began to choke, when a bit of the bread got caught in her throat. Quickly, she reached for her water glass, taking a deep drink. As soon as she came up for air, she began to sputter. Raven felt as if she had hit a raw nerve with the elder lady.

"How did you find that name, Raven? This name has only been known by those on the Piedmont. It has a long line of ancestry, tracing, at least, two hundred years. Did you find something in that mound? I had a feeling you would find something in there. I did not follow you all, because I am extremely claustrophobic. But, I do know of this Pond name. Please tell me first how you came across it in that mound."

Thomasina's hands were visibly shaking now. Maybe the proof that she knew something.

"We found a manuscript rolled into a baton, with a creature modelled on top. As we were going through the cairn, we saw writing everywhere. It was when we went to the main chamber of the cairn, that we found the baton, still clasped in the skeletal hand of a long dead woman," Raven looked solid at her aunt. She could see that the elder lady was whispering a name, over and over.

"You found Martiz didn't you? By all the earths, everyone that ever was since her disappearance has been trying to find her. You mean she was in my backyard all along? Did you find Kem and the two younger children as well? Oh my, oh my, you all might have found a way to beat this thing that has followed you to the island. She was here in the Piedmont two hundred years ago.

Her story was told and retold. First by her son Tennif Pond, then his children, their children, and on and on until it reached Ravenna, your mother. Yes, she is a descendant of Martiz. She was her sixth grandmother. Even though the strain of the Waddis was thin, it played havoc with her physicality. That is why her parents sent her to live on the Piedmont, with her grandparents. Unlike anyone else of her family, she alone carried the genes of the strongest points of the Waddis. They would have killed her in the flatlands," The elder lady took Raven's face within her hands, almost committing it to memory. They stayed that way for a while, until she finally let go, dropping into her seat.

"By all that breathes. You have found the lost letter of Martiz. Her son, Tennif Pond, tried to find the domed hideaway that her and her husband Kem had built here on the Piedmont. He found the cairn in the back here, but there was no way to get in, until Raven stumbled on it. My loves, you have opened up your history, family history that is. Seth, Raven, you are descendants of this great lady. Yes, that means you have Waddis swimming in your bodies. I know it has been five or more generations since, none the less, it is still there. Your mother Ravenna, carried the genes to the both of you. Unlike human genes, the Waddis genes tend to take over the human parts at times. Like the time you broke your foot, Seth. How long did it take to heal?" Thomasina reached out her hands to Seth, imploring him to remember the incident.

"Yes, I do remember that, aunt. It took no more than two days to heal. When I asked Momma and Papa about it, they would not answer me. Finally, Momma said that I was a strong boy, and drank my milk every day. According to her, that was how my foot mended so fast. She would always hug me and kiss me really hard on my cheek, when I would ask her of this. I never thought anything more until now. Does that mean my sister and I are freaks?" Seth began to shake so hard, he dropped his sandwich into his lap.

"No, my love it does not. It just means that your inheritance is much more than you have ever known. I remember, when you were small, you asked your Momma where she came from, who were her ancestors. She answered as I recall, *"Child,we will speak about this later."* She never varied her answer. I think she was trying to protect you from your ancestors. If the Waddis were to catch you, they would soon find out what you are. They could manipulate your genes to turn on themselves. In one case, you would perish. In the other case, you would metamorphosis into one of them. All the while, your brain would still be Seth. In both cases, it is a death sentence. We must be careful that neither you nor your sister comes in contact with them. The fragment here is so broken, nothing can come through it and live. They can not make it here, on any of the continents or islands on this earth. But, it seems that something has attached itself to your boat. I have been told that it only attacks organic life, such as ourselves. We need to put into plan what to do. As long as you stay out of the water, you will be safe. Bernis, may I have the letter to read please?" Thomasina reached to receive the baton from Bernis.

Bernis got to thinking, "We came here through a fragment on the ocean where your boat was. That is why you could only see half of our bodies. So there must be something powering the fragment so it can only be used from one specific point to the other. When I was with the chain gang, our starting point was always home world for the Waddis. We walked through the fragment from there, through your boat, which led to the mines on the Challaque mountains.

I think they might be on earth seven, because every time we went there the Sargent Major would always repeat *"number seven"* three times before we made our way through the fragment. So, whatever power is used, it needs a verbal command to make it work. I do not know what that would be, because we always were transported in the dark," he sat back down upon the pillow, trying to think of anything he might have seen in the Waddis home world that linked itself to dimensional travel in only one path.

Thomasina read the letter from the baton carefully. Tears and sobs took part as she read it slowly, so she could understand every word. For almost two centuries the Pond family had searched for anything about Martiz and her family. Descendants into descendants had searched the Piedmont, not realising that it was right here all along. There were those that felt the family found a fragment, getting swept up in it to another earth or even home world. It was baffling that it had remained unknown for so long.

The elder lady sat back in her chair, thinking about the latter. Reaching to get the baton, she accidentally dropped it. A small round object dropped out of the baton. She hurriedly picked everything up, to see what had happened when she had dropped it. The filial of the Urtus was still in its place on the top latch of the baton. She took a cloth napkin, putting it on her lap, spread out flat for the purpose she needed it for. With the paper in hand, she placed the round object on the napkin. Then she upended the baton, to see if anything else was in there. Something that looked like a black rock fell on the napkin, then another round object. Shaking the baton a bit did not loosen anything else within the tube. All the eyes in the room were staring at the objects, covered with rust or dirt so it could not be told what they were at the moment. Thomasina took out a small paintbrush that she used to debug her roses. Its bristles weren't stiff, and had enough flexibility not to do any damage. She carefully began to apply the brush to one of the round objects. Little flecks of dirt fell into her lap. The round objects turned out to be rings. One ring had a solid blue stone, like a turquoise. The other ring was solid gold. On the facet in the top of it was cut a set of initials, M and K, both in capitals. The odd black rock proved to be the most interesting of the group. When all the dirt was taken away, the object was still quite heavy. The elderly lady took a smooth cloth that was in her apron pocket. She rubbed the object until it came forth. It was an old parchment sealer. In the old days,people did not have envelopes and such. Sometimes they rolled up what was written into a scroll. Sometimes it was folded in neat corners for the recipient to open.

Both items were sealed with a large drop of wax. On that wax, the person sending the item, pushed their seal upon the wax, leaving a design that was all their own. The drama on the seal was very simple indeed. It had two Utrus, face to face in an upward stance. The barbs on their tails could be clearly seen, despite the age of the seal. Martiz's family had something to do with the little beasts. Besides didn't Seth find a part of a tail that he tried to clear the first plinth with? According to Bernis, they still used the Utrus in managing their countless number of slaves. No one, not even the Waddis wanted to tangle with one. A good guess would say they were bred by one particular group or family. Could Martiz's family be a colony of breeders for these devilish things?

Thomasina stood up. She had the parchment seal, which was actually a ring, as well as the other two rings. She handed them to Raven, because she had small hands. Seth would not be able to fit any of these on his thick fingers. He was OK to let her have them. They would definitely get in the way of the nets. The elder lady took the notes that Seth had made of the star map. She noticed that this earth was not of worm hole or fragment contained. But there was access to the home world through a trans-dimensional fragment leading to earth seven,and the mines on Challaque. A trans-dimensional fragment is formed by device, not by nature bound. Someone had the knowhow to make a device like this. Whether Waddis or human born, there was clues that it did exist in the Waddis home world. Bernis' memories of that place were more than likely controlled. No one was allowed to see the device. The miner prisoners always left at night, hence Raven seeing them at three minutes past midnight, while on the boat. To access the fragment, they had to get back on the boat, going to the same location where they found Bernis. It would take at least, two hours, so they had to leave soon.

Thomasina stood up, handing the star map back to Seth, "We will make lunch, and all of us, including me will ride on Titan. He will fly us to the boat, remaining there with me. Raven, come with me. I have something more to give you."

She handed a golden rope to lace the seal through, so she could carry it around her neck. She wore the blue stone ring on her left hand, and the inscribed ring, she wore on her right hand. These were worn around the middle finger of both hands. The elder lady felt that these signs of ancestry might be a good thing to wear when they rode the boat to where the fragment was. She felt it could, actually, save their lives.

Raven went to help Bernis to make the food they were taking.

Seth went over to see what Thomasina wanted. The elder lady was motioning him to come close to her, "Outstretch your hand, my love." As he did that, she placed the baton into his hand, "Carry this with you. I feel we might be able to use it. It might mean that we can return from this alive," she kissed her nephew on the cheek, hugging him as she did.

Seth tucked the baton into a strap he always wore. It hooked itself from the front of his belt to the back. Primarily he used it to help him pull his fishing nets in. He would use the clamp on the tying end of the net, hooking it onto his strap, giving him the extra strength he needed to pull the heavy nets in. Raven always helped, but the strap had also helped him time and again. He knew that the baton would not shift from where he put it.

Titan knew something was up. He waggled all around the yard, bellowing and honking as he did.

When Thomasina brought out his harness, he stamped his webbed feet in anticipation. Even he was thoroughly devoted to the elder lady, he did like a bit of adventure was afoot, as far as food was involved. Raven and Bernis got all the food ready to take, making they had enough for several days. They got all the empty jugs they could find, filling them once they got to the shore.

Seth hoped that Father Damien and Evangeline were still near the boat dock, as well as the two stalwart men that helped them into their boat so they would not touch the contamination that surrounded his and Raven's boat. He was glad they already off loaded the fish. Hopefully the cold box was where they could get it. He did not worry about his friends, but there were unsavoury types on all coasts. You just had to be careful. All the food was loaded in cold chests that Bernis attached to Titan's harness.

There was only two saddles on the gander's back, so Seth and Bernis would have to wedge themselves somewhere between the women. There was room enough, but to stay aloft was the main concern.

"OK, Raven, you will ride in the second saddle behind me. Seth, you will sit behind Raven, holding onto her because she will be belted in. Bernis, you will sit behind me, doing the same thing that Seth is doing with Raven."

Thomasina knew Titan well, and was not worried about the flight. Seth and Raven were not nervous about the ride either. However, Bernis had never done this, hoping that his nerves would not get the better of him.

With a great swooshing sound, Titan lifted off of the side of the Piedmont. His large wings stretched out at his sides as he glided through the updrafts that came from the mountain.

Everyone could see the coast a little ways from them. As Bernis looked down, he felt two small hands encircle his waist. He knew then that he had nothing to fear. They would soon be circling the coast.

Titan bellowed into the air stream. His gander sound was larger than the others that answered him. All the other geese could do was follow with their eyes and honk their approval. Titan was the only Largess Gander Goose on this earth. There were others of his kind on earth two, but that was too much of a fragment away. The Largess gander made his circling approach of their landing area in the dunes near the coast. Titan landed soft as baby down. Everyone was astonished to find out that they had landed. They were still in their seats. Bernis noticed that Raven still held his waist. He put his large hand over hers, as a silent thank you. She did not know, at this time, how that simple gesture was important to him. It had been a long time since he had any human outside contact. Where he was imprisoned on Waddis home world, no contact was allowed. Not even eye contact was attempted for the fear of the contemptible Urtus. He had heard many a story about them from the Waddis themselves, but he had never seen it happen by his eyes.

Thomasina hopped off of Titan. She landed into the soft sand of the dunes. Bernis followed her, landing feet first on the sand, sinking in up to his knees in sand. Raven and Seth jumped down, helping their friend out of the dune. For a short time their laughter drove away any fears they might have had.

When they were all assembled, they started to take the food baskets down, so they could load them on the jetty boat that would take them to their boat, still sitting on the dark patch of water off of the coast.

Thomasina went to speak to Father Damien and Evangeline, to catch up with what was going on. Bernis and Seth set to go to the community spigot, where they could fill all of their water jugs. They would need this as well as the food on their journey. The dock keeper let them use his wagon to truck the water to the jetty boat.

Once they all got the supplies on the jetty boat, Seth remembered the cold box for the fish they would catch later. Evangeline came running to the jetty boat, pulling a wagon behind her, loaded with the cold box for the fish.

"I couldn't have done it without you Evangeline," Seth said as he loaded the cold box onto the front of the jetty boat. The young woman bowed her head, her cheeks showing a bright blush.

"Not a problem, Seth. Do you want me to deposit your pay into the bank for you, like always?" Evangeline was still blushing. Seth took her hand, and kissed it.

"Always, my lady. Thank you for your help. I hope to see you when everything is said and done," Seth said softly, knowing that he could always charm this girl.

The jetty drivers pushed the boat to where it was just tipping into the water. They quickly climbed into the jetty boat, all the while keeping their eyes on the growing darkness underneath Seth,and Raven's boat. Titan obediently flew to the boat to await his mistress. If they could not leave the boat by normal means,they could, at least, leave by Largess Gander goose.

Everything was loaded safely onto Seth and Raven's boat. Thomasina and Raven worked on stowing away the food, while Bernis took in all the water jugs, plus the cold box with the help of the jetty men.

Seth noticed some nets that he forgot about on the deck, and set forth to stowing them away for now. Bernis placed the cold box in its cradle. As he finished this, he peered over the side of the boat to the now undulating darkness, that stretched over its keel.

"Seth, come here! There are faces within the darkness under the boat. They look human to me," Bernis was none the less startled at what he was witnessing. He frantically waved at Seth to come over and see it for himself.

Seth calmly walked over to where Bernis was. The man pointed to shapes within the darkened water. He looked long and hard to see what Bernis saw. In a fluid moment he saw people swim through the darkness, trying to make it to the surface. It frightened him so that he fainted on the deck. He had been keeping too much in until this time, and it got the better of him.

Bernis took a cup of water, and splashed it on Seth's forehead. The cool water had the desired effect. He woke up immediately, sputtering the water that had dripped to his mouth when he sat up. Looking at Bernis, he could see the caring in his eyes. How he wished he could feel that. He had always relied on Raven to show emotions. This was his one gift from the Waddis. Bernis helped him to his feet. Standing up, he saw his sister and aunt, looking very worried about him. They, among all the others; knew how he was. They should understand.

With an unsteady gait, Seth walked towards his room, under the deck of the boat. He needed to find his charts, so they could go to exactly where they had been when they first encountered Bernis and the other half men. The sun was still high in the sky, they would have time to make it there. He would make sure that they would be there on time.

He knew what important was, despite his lack of proper emotions. If they hadn't found the cairn, he would still believe that he was like his mother. She never smiled, but you could tell that she loved you with a look of her jet black eyes, just like Raven's. It was a legacy that she didn't like to talk about. It was there, none the less. Grabbing his navigation charts, he walked up the stairs to the top deck. Raven waited for him at the top stair.

"Seth, are you alright? You had me worried when you fainted. That's not happened to you since Mama died. If you need Bernis and I to take this mission over, we gladly will. Tell me what you want us to do, and it will be done," Raven took his hand and led him towards a large deck chair. Their father used to sit in it while the boat was in still water, as they were now. The chair had been bolted to the deck, for safety, years ago. Seth reminded her of their father, who not so long ago, sat here. She helped unfurl and keep the pages from blowing away as he read them.

"The west wind is picking up. Bernis, if you could help me with the sails, Raven can take the rudder until we are done. First,we have to take up the anchor. Can you help me with that? I am still a little shaky," Seth said and got up slowly, pacing himself to make it to the mast.

As Bernis was rolling up the anchor chain on the wench, he slowly started to furl the sails.

"OK, you sit down, friend. I can do the sails. Just tell me which one and which way. You are still a bit weak. Thomasina is brewing everyone a stout cup of tea, we all might need it. I asked Titan to sit beside you. He makes a noise, a waggling noise, that soothes. Please take my word for it," Bernis said as he helped Seth to the chair, Titan was already waiting for him. The waggling had already begun.

While Seth was directing Bernis with the sails, Raven was minding the rudder. She knew which way to go to where they would find the home world manufactured fragment. Sitting there, watching the two men work together, she went back within her mind. She could only do this when she was alone. Strange as it was, she could still manage the rudder as she entered her innermost thoughts. The only way to see that she was doing it would be to look at her eyes. There was no white in her eyes, only the liquid black darkness contained within her iris and pupils. The men were too busy to look at her.

Could it be that Raven had a bit of a glimmer of feelings for Bernis? Yes, she did put her arms around him when they were on Titan, but that was only to keep him stable, since he did not have a saddle. She liked the way he helped others, without question. She knew that he had suffered a great deal under the hands of the Waddis. Would he hold it against her that she was descendant from a high princess? Ah, they had only known each other for a day and a half, almost two days. This was not enough time to set your life on a given course. She went deeper into her mind, thinking of her parents. Trying to see where the landmarks were in their behavior. Someone was calling her name.

"Raven? Do they have you all the way back here on the rudder? Here, I brought you some hot tea with lemon. I grow the tea myself on the sides of the Piedmont. Here dear, take it, you will need it for this trip," Thomasina held the cup out for her to take.

As Raven lifted her head, her eyes had gone back to their normal way. Taking the cup from her aunt, she sat it down in a small curved spot that Seth had made so they could keep their cups there from falling off.

"Thank you, auntie. This is much needed. I was getting a little sleepy," She said and gave her aunt a small kiss on the cheek, as she bent down to hug her.

"Do not dare to show those coal blacks like your Momma's. I loved her as much as I love you. If certain people see you this way, they might run away from you for good! I love you, child. I do not want anything bad to happen to you. That is why I am here. Here, drink your tea. I put my special ingredient for you, to make you feel better," Thomasina said and released her hug, standing over her niece, glad that the darkness had flown from her eyes. If they survived this mission, she would need to start to teach Raven what was called "The Way". It would be then she would understand the true gift she had.

"Aunt, is there ash bark in the tea? I can taste its floral. Thank you so much for making this special tea for me. I have always loved it, and you. Yes ma'am, I will duly watch what I do. I do like Bernis a lot. He is a good man. I just do not know where this is going to lead us. Thank you for being my aunt," Raven got up and hugged her aunt, kissing her on her already tear stained cheeks.

Thomasina brought a cup of the tea to both Seth and Bernis, who had just finished burnishing the sails. Bernis sat beside Titan,who the elder lady had brought some carrots to eat, perfectly shredded. She sat on Titan's back, watching the way the sails furled out with the wind, taking them to a destination that no one knew what would happen, once they reached there.

Hopefully they would be at the exact spot where Raven had seen the half men.

Half in their earth and half in the fragment manufactured by someone or something on the Waddis home world.

Titan started to waggle very loud, almost barking into the breeze that surrounded the boat, pushing them forward into their destinies. It was almost as if the Largess gander goose, could see and smell something they could not. Thomasina started to stroke his grey feathered head, to try to soothe him. It would not be had. He continued to waggle his loudest, trying to make his mistress understand what was bothering him. The elder lady did what only she could do with her goose. She placed her hands on his large head, right behind his eyeballs. She had to concentrate very hard to do this, and it always took her energy, all of her energy to key this in.

Thomasina rubbed her palms together to get a static. She then put the left and the right, behind Titan's eyeballs.

Pressing lightly, she could feel his worry coming through. The swirls of color were very intense as she walked further within his mind. She had always felt that the gander had been a human once, many years ago. As far as the way he was changed, she could never reach that far in his memory. Maybe he did not want her to go back into his past. Baring her way into where she needed to go, she saw her first clue. In her vision, she could see the goose surrounded by tall, snaking Waddis. The sparse hair on their heads made them look even more sinister. The large, owl-like eyes rolled within their sockets. Their elongated fingers stroked the goose' grey feathers in random patterns. They hissed like snakes. It made cold chills go up and down her spine. She could not tell what they were trying to do. The elder lady only knew that, whatever they were doing, it was upsetting Titan.

The Largess gander did not flinch or make a move in the waking world. All he did was waggle, bleat, and cry for help. Thomasina pressed harder behind his eyes, trying not to press too hard, or it would kill him. In the world of his mind, she got closer to be able to see just what was going on. The Waddis had disappeared into the mist of his mind scape. All she could see now was just Titan, and there was a man, dressed in grey, standing behind him. The man made no moves at all. But, there was so much sadness on his face, it almost made her cry. She called out to the man, "I am Thomasina, friend of Titan, the Largess gander goose, who are you? Can I help you in any way?"

The man just looked at her, mournfully sad. He began to open his mouth, not very wide, because his teeth were clenched in terror. His hand came up to motion the elder lady to come closer.

As she did, Thomasina could hear him whisper, "I am Titan." She almost jumped back within Titan's mind and back into the world of reality. If she had done that, the Largess gander goose would be no more. She did not want to loose her trusted friend. What sparked his memory? How could a man be changed into a goose? A rather large goose at that. She decided to go no further for now. Where ever the memory existed within his brain, it would still be there when she came back at another time.

"I will be back, man of Titan. You have my word on it," Thomasina reached towards the grey man, touching his fingers, then left the mind of her friend. She knew that he had left something within her with his simple touch. She would keep it to herself to think about later. Her feelings were at a curve, a high curve. It was time to stop. She took her hands off from behind Titan's eyes. Then she kissed him on the head, petting his dense feathers. The gander opened his eyes to look at his mistress. He droned a low waggle, soothing himself and her as well.

Seth turned to his aunt, "Is everything OK, Thomasina? You had me worried for a bit there. The words that came out of your mouth sounded like a man's voice. Can we talk about this later?" He put his arm around his aunt. She shook her head in agreement, squeezing both of his hands when she did.

"Nephew, I have to tend to dinner now. Would you have Titan sit with you until that time? He is OK for now, but he needs to cool off from his experience. When we have dinner, I want you to sit by me so we can discuss this matter," Thomasina took Seth into her embrace, kissing him on the cheek. She did the same to Titan before she left to go to the kitchen.

Raven held fast to the rudder. She had promised Thomasina that she would not turn her eyes inward while so visible. Where she could do it, she did not know. Perhaps when everyone was asleep, and wouldn't have eyes open to see her. She watched the sails catch the afternoon wind. Soon the men would huddle, pouring over the star charts that Bernis had dictated to Seth within the cairn of Martiz and Kem. Thoughts wandered to that far away time when Martiz and Kem had their romance. How much of the Waddis did her brother and herself inherit? She knew how her brother had always been, never once connecting it to the Waddis. As for herself, she knew what that was. The eyes have it.

Bernis walked over to where Raven was on the rudder, "Could you use some help or company? Seth said he would call me if he needed me. Titan is sitting with him, to keep him company. I have a question to ask you and it can be answered or not. Was Titan ever anything else than a rather large gander goose? Your aunt, Thomasina, was talking to him while she travelled through, carbon based. With that as the base and a little know how, it can be done. Who or whatever it was done to, always suffered. I have seen the ones that they changed from beast to man. They did not know how to act or communicate, always suffering the self doubt of who they really were. It was sad."

"I do not know of this. The best person to ask is my aunt Thomasina. I have always known Titan as full grown. She told my brother and I that he came to this earth on the tail of a fragment. To her, he looked like he had just hatched. His feathers were all downy, and he still had his egg tooth. The fragment he came through, she had never seen before, and some was attached to him. She said that the fragment almost looked man made.

She has had Titan with her, at least, twenty years that I know of," Raven said as she picked up her cup to drink the last drams that clung to the bottom.

Chapter Four

"So, where did you and your brother live while he was growing up on the island?" Bernis questioned as he leaned against a railing that was near where Raven sat.

"We mostly lived on the ocean with Papa. Mama liked to stay on land. Our house was located on the continent of Tasvale, not far from the island. Sometimes when there are clouds hiding the sun, you can see a small reflection of the continent from the island, and visa versa. My brother took over the fishing route when Papa's arthritis became too much for him. When Mama died, Papa took me to the island. We lived with Thomasina for a while, in the old Pond house. It was close enough for all of us to be together daily. I love the old Pond house. Anyone connected with it, including Thomasina, always worked on the cottage to keep it liveable. I think she always wished me or my brother would live there. It would be nice. I don't mind helping Seth while I can," Raven recounted and rocked back in her chair, as the memories filled her mind.

"Losing your parents must have been hard. My father died young, and my mother dies when the Waddis took over my earth. I think about them every day, even if it is just for a little bit," Bernis said and stood up, listening to Seth calling for him, leaning down to pat Raven on the shoulder as he left. They came face to face, so close it would make you shiver. Seth called again, so Bernis took off to help, turning back once to smile at Raven.

"Guard your spirit girl," Raven heard with her heart dancing tiptoe around her vitals within. The man certainly had what she wanted. The thing between that was, if they survived what they had contrived to do. If and only if they survived, then the rest of their lives could continue.

She wondered if Titan and Thomasina had a past other than what they had now. Suddenly, she heard her brother shouting to her. His pitch was shrill, something had happened. She tied out the rudder so it could stay on course, sprinting towards where she heard the sound of her brother's pleading.

Seth did not know what to do. Bernis had jumped overboard because he thought he had seen one of his friends trying to swim towards the boat. He had jumped so far out, that the blackness under the boat did not catch him. Fruitlessly, you could see him swimming around the boat. Indeed he was a powerful swimmer, but even the most powerful would tire out after time.

Titan was honking and squawking loudly towards where Bernis was swimming. By chance, Raven looked eastward. There was something swimming towards the boat.

The darkness underneath sensed the swimmer. She could see skinny arms flailing at the water, trying to make it. Raven knew what had to be done. She took ahold of Titan's back where Thomasina had left her saddle. She levered herself into it, grabbing for a large fishnet with a long handle.

"Titan, hup hup!" She shouted it as loud as she could, so Thomasina could hear it where she was in the galley, cooking. The elder lady put all of the cooking food to the side, dashing out of the galley door to see if she could help. As she made it to the deck, she saw Raven on top of Titan. The Largess gander goose was fluttering his wings into flight. Within seconds he was in the air.

"By the spirits that guide us, please keep Raven safe," Thomasina said to herself as she watched her niece guiding the goose to first catch the frail looking person that was trying to make it to the boat, unaware of the darkness underneath.

Raven took the handle of the net, fastening a rope that was attached to it, to her waist. She held up the net to snag the person up out of the water. In one swoop, the person was caught. He did not struggle in the net, for he could see how hard this girl was working to save him. Titan flew over the boat, hovering enough to let the person down into the waiting arms of Seth and Thomasina. For her to catch Bernis would be a little tricky. Bernis had stopped swimming, because he was watching Raven save his friend. He knew that Titan would have to fly low enough for him to catch hold of one of his feet, then fly him to the boat. Raven had something else in mind. She seemed to think she could save Bernis the same way that she saved the other man.

What she failed to do was to take into consideration the weight difference of the two men. The first man was almost a skeleton, he was so thin. Bernis, on the other hand, was a muscular man with some weight on his bones, knew all to well what needed to be done.

The man looked for which way Titan was flying. He did as most geese and large birds tend to do, a few hard flaps, then a silken glide. Bernis estimated he would be "on glide" while he passed over him. He got Raven's attention that he was going to grab onto one of Titan's feet, hoping he would not shake him off. Through hand signals he got her to understand how he would do it. He could see that she was leaning on the gander's neck. It almost looked as if she was telling him what to do.

The Largess gander goose flapped his wings, nearly touching the surface of the water.

After the one action, he was already gliding. Bernis was ready. The gander passed over as he took all of his strength to almost jump out of the water, catching Titan's lower leg. The bird did not flinch. It was as if he had been commanded to do what he was doing. Bernis climbed up his large leg. When he got to where the feathers were, he would grasp hand holds of feathers, moving up with his feet as an anchor. When he made it to the goose's broad back, he collapsed behind Raven. She took the rope that was attached to the net, tying him onto the saddle she sat on, if in case he would fall over.

Titan had to fly around in a circle over the boat until he saw the right place to land. As he landed, Bernis woke up, scrambling to sit behind Raven as she stayed in Thomasina's saddle. He put his arms around her waist, as she had done his, for the landing.

The Largess gander goose landed as soft as silk in the middle of the boat. Raven and Bernis stayed on his back until he settled to sit, while Thomasina petted him, letting him know what a good goose he was. Seth helped Raven down first, hugging her as she stood on the deck. It startled her, because he had never hugged her before. She saw a tear leave his eye, flowing down his cheek. She wiped it with the back of her hand, kissing his cheek a she did.

Bernis had to be helped down from Titan. He had strained a leg muscle with all of his climbing. Seth and Raven helped him down. He hugged them both in a hearty thank you. The skin and bones that Raven had rescued first was sitting on a large coil of rope. When Bernis walked over to him, he realised he did not know the man at all.

"Sir, who you be?" Bernis asked while looking at all the bones tentatively covered with thin, blotched skin. The head was down, not coming up. Bernis reached under the chin, trying to move all the dreadlocks out of view of the face. When he finally saw the face, he froze. Ice water found its way into his veins.

"You are a Waddis! Why be you here?" Horrified, he let the head slack down again, wanting to run from this being. He wanted to wash his whole body after touching this thing before him.

Slowly, the head came up on its own. The bloodshot bulging eyes cast their cold, blue eyed stare around the humans assembled on the deck. The eyes stopped at Titan, waggling to himself already. The thin lips opened, "Yes, I was born a Waddis, artificially conceived and raised within a laboratory. We grow up very fast in the laboratory. Within two years, I was ready for release. I was going to be trained under the gaze of the highest leader of the home world, Leonic.

After serving him for ten earth years, I was evacuated to an earth post, here, under the guise of being human. My job was to research the humans here, to report back to Leonic on a monthly basis. Since I was alone, I became very attached to this earth and its people. In fact,I became so attached, I fell in love with a human woman. Her name was Ruby. In her kindness, she befriended me, as my look was transfigured to be more human than Waddis. One night, when Ruby and I were sitting in her home, talking; there was a sound at the door. The Waddis Council was at the door. They broke it down, killing my beautiful human! I was taken to adjudication, where I was penalized with enemy consortium, and assigned to prison. There I stayed for so many years I lost count. Then came my release. I was told to join the half men, who went through the fragment to another earth to the mines. I did this for some years.

I walked behind you, Bernis. Yes, now you see me! My name is Thomas. Do you remember now how I was not fed, and you gave me half of your food? Something like that is never forgotten my friend. Because of my starvation I lost my human looks, except for this hair," he said as he ran his bony hands through it.

Everyone was rendered speechless. Bernis found his words, knowing that this one being could help them find the fragment, to try free the slaves there. The fragment would be destroyed, but how?

"How did you get here? We must find out how you got out of the fragment, whether man made or not. Can you help us?"

"I would be glad to, over a cup of that marvelous soup someone is cooking in the galley," Thomas looked around to see an astonished Thomasina,who had forgotten about her soup, with all this mayhem that was going on.

Within minutes the elder lady had a steaming bowl of her vegetable soup ready for Thomas to drink.

"Here you go sir. I always keep a pot of stew on the back burner of my stove. I am ever so glad that you smelled it, because I had moved the temperature up, and forgotten about it. I brought you a couple slices of crusty bread, to dip with, of course," she said and handed the tray to Thomas, blushing as he took it in his hands.

"Thank you kindly my lady. My Ruby used to make a soup similar to this when we were together. Ah, what times there were! Now, to discuss the fragment, I will be glad to. I expect that you, Bernis and you. I do not know your name yet. But, here, have a seat and we will get to the heart of the matter. The goose can listen, too. He understands everything, you know. Titan hadn't always been a goose. I knew him when he was a man,"

Thomas said before ripping off a large hunk of bread, dipping it into the soup. Hungrily, he ate it while smiling. Good way to start a dialogue, he thought to himself.

Everyone was quiet. What they had thought had been revealed. Thomasina especially. She knew that this talk would have to wait. Oh but the agony of the wait!

Thomasina and Raven left the men to discuss the plot. Raven went to her rudder, Thomasina to the kitchen to finish lunch. By the way we breathe and speak, let this be a fruitful way of getting to the right place.

While in her enclave with the rudder, Raven prayed long and hard. Her Papa had taught her to pray. He was such a good man. How she missed him. While stationing the rudder, she felt a thud and a cracking sound coming from under the rudder.

She called for Seth, he knew this boat in all its ways. Bernis and Thomas were left to continue on the discussion of what could be done to thwart the Waddis.

Seth looked over the railing directly beneath the rudder. As he pulled it up,he could see that the rudder was fine, except for some seaweed that attached itself to it. That, in itself was unusual. Seaweed, on this earth, would only be found closer to the coastlands and beaches. So where did this seaweed come from? Toland island was already a good distance from where they were now. Enough time and travel to escape the seaweed beds near the reefs that bordered the shore of the island. Seth took a stick he had handy, pulled the seaweed off, and deposited it over the side of the boat. The rudder had no cracks, so he put it back into position.

"Raven, I do not feel good about this. When I looked over the side the darkness, somehow, looked much darker that it had been earlier. I am going into the belly to check for anything. You stay here by the rudder, we need all the manpower we got to make it to our destination. I will get back with you when I come back up," Seth said and turned to go into the belly of the ship where his room was located. He hoped that all he would see would be ropes and nets, saying a prayer to himself as he walked away.

Thomas and Bernis were deep into the discussion of the Waddis made fragment that would go from the home world to earth seven and the mines.

"Do you think that a human manufactured fragment?" Bernis asked as he poured over the star chart that he had directed Seth to make.

Thomas sipped the rest of the soup out of his bowl.

"Within a shadow of a doubt, my tall friend. I even heard before I left the mines that there was a sort of rebellion going on in home world. The younger Waddis are tired of the dictatorship of the old order Waddis. They want to move forward, away from the slaves doing their work. They would much rather depend on new technology. I only overheard this in passing by the Waddis guard post as I went to serve my time in the mines. Soon after that I found my way out of there."

"How did you do such a thing? I did not think it was even close to getting out of the mines to freedom," Bernis scratched his head, trying to think of different ways to get out of that mine. The daylight came into his eyes, reminding him that there was a hole in the vault of the mine. You had to look really fast to see it, because the Waddis were always hurrying them into the belly of the mine. That hole was big enough for a body to get through, especially the skin and bones of Thomas.

"The way out was easier than I thought. I just kept walking into the mine, no one paid me no interest as I walked away from the other slaves, into the darkness of the mine. My instinct told me to keep walking straight. You see, Waddis have more of a magnetic core that humans do. We can find our way out of almost anything. I never heard my name called, so I kept walking. Soon, I came to a small stream in the back of the mine. I followed the flow of the stream to where it went out of a hole of daylight. It was just big enough to squeeze my bones through it. When I came out, I saw a thin piece of fragment, flapping me in the face. I reached to hold it, and it took me here. I have been staying on a small island just right over there. Kept myself alive with fish and coconuts. Then it came to where I saw your boat. So, I took a chance, swimming over here. This part of the ocean is too cold for the ridged sharks, so I knew I had a chance," Thomas finished and put his soup bowl down beside him. The story was real indeed. Was he?

Bernis took all this into consideration. He now remembered the half fleshed man he would share his rations with. Thankful he was that they found one another. But what of the fragment that took him from the mines to here? Could that be used to save his comrades? He took up Thomas' bowl and spoon with a promise to bring some back. He headed to the galley, asking Thomasina to take another bowl to Thomas. He had not seen Seth anywhere. He walked over to where Raven was, asking her where her brother was. She told him of the sound they heard, and that Seth had left to check into the belly of the ship, but had not come back yet.

Bernis gave her a kiss on the cheek, taking off towards the stairs that led down below.

"Seth are you down here?" He shouted as he jumped over the stairs to the floor. A low groan was coming from where Seth had set up his bedroom, after Raven had joined him. Walking fast over to where he heard the moan, he saw Seth, bloodied, on the floor. There was an iron pipe next to his head.

Bernis knew by seeing this that the perpetrator could be close by. Slowly he tuned around so he could see every corner. In the last corner, near the cold box for the fish, he saw a figure. The figure was short, small in stature. Much like the skin and bones of Thomas. He took down the lantern that hung by him. Thankfully it was lit, but very low in fuel. Shining the lantern at the corner, he saw what looked like a child. But, this was no child he had ever seen before. The face was lined with wrinkles and scars. Its eyes were large and globular, much like a Waddis, but not truly.

He decided to ask a question of the being, who was clenching and unclenching its fists. He could hear the creature grind his teeth so much, that it looked as if pieces of teeth flew out of its mouth.

"Please be, who are you and what do you need?" He asked the being, hoping for a quick answer.

Raven was sitting by the rudder, making sure it had them go where they needed to. The sails looked good for now. If it was left up to her, she could do it. Almost as sudden she realised, "Oh my, we left Tulli at the cottage! I must tie the rudder, and go see if Thomasina will let Titan go get him. I am so stupid to leave my own dog. He must be scared!"

She steadied the rudder, running to the galley where Thomasina was.

The elder lady met her at the door, "Don't worry my sweet. I have already sent Titan to get him. He should be back within the hour.

I had only realised it myself, when I heard you shouting outside. Don't worry, Raven. Tulli is a very smart dog. He will wait at the cottage until he is properly collected. Now, here's a cup of stew for you and Thomasina. I put some crusty bread in a bag. There's enough for the both of you. You must stay on the rudder, to make sure that we go straight, my love."

Thomasina kissed Raven on the cheek, handing her the bag of bread, which she hung on her arm. Raven dropped off her soup and bread at the little cup hook near her chair, carrying the remainder to Thomasina. When she went there, the creature was not there. She left his stew and bread beside where he had been sitting. Looking all around, she did not see the thing. She knew Bernis was checking on Seth. *"Maybe he followed him down,"* she thought.

Thomasina stepped softly upon the stairs leading down to the belly of the boat. She had heard Bernis upon entering. It sounded almost like he was speaking to someone, not Seth. His Waddis core was ringing hard, pushing him further. By that core, he could feel that all was not right. As he reached the bottom of the stairs, the core had told him well. Standing before him was Bernis talking to what he referred to as a "shadow" from home world. This could get tricky.

Thomasina almost stammered as she began to speak, "Excuse me Bernis. Can you please take care of Seth? I see he is in need of attention. Do not worry, these little minks bark is much more than their bite. I will take care of our new guest," she stepped forward in front of where Bernis was standing. As soon as he was set, Bernis moved to help Seth, who was trying to get up.

"Little shadow, are you hurt or angered about something?" Thomasina asked as she bent her knees, making herself the same height of the creature, eye to eye, "I will help you with anything you need, little one. Just tell me what it is."

The creature stepped a bit forward. The clenched fists were now limp by its sides. The teeth grinding had disappeared, ending the look of all the wrinkles. Even though it still had wrinkles, they were not as much awesome as they were before.

"Come and tell me what you need, little one," Thomasina said as she raised her right hand to the creature.

What came next was a pitch of speech so high, that it hurt human ears. Thomas motioned for Bernis to help Seth up the stairs. He then turned back to the creature waiting for it to reply.

"I am a fifth form shadow, sir. I can see that you are a Waddis of a different type. You have head hair! I have not seen that phenomenon in many a year kind sir. I hope that I did nothing to truly hurt the human. I was afraid for myself. I fell into this boat when it was not moving. There was no one here, so I went to this place that you see, and arranged a place for me to sleep," The shadow gestured at the pile of clothing that it had bunched together to make a sleeping place. From the look of the clothing, they were actually Seth's, not the shadow's. Thomasina decided to leave that for now.

"Come with me shadow. We can see if the human you hit is OK. I am sure you are hungry. But, please, do not speak when we go on deck until I warn the humans. Their ears are too sensitive for your voice," Thomasina said as she took the shadow's hand, leading him into the sunlit bathed upper deck.

Seth was fine, just some bruising on his head, and a cut lip, and hands. Raven was busy cleaning him up when the shadow made his appearance on the deck. Thomas whispered something in the creature's ear. He shook his head in agreement. Slowly, Thomas took him over to Seth. He first warned Seth of the high caliber vocals shadows have, and to cup his hands over his ears. He motioned for the rest to do the same.

The shadow opened his mouth, ever so small, "I am sorry that I hurt you sir. I was afraid for my own life. I fell into your ship from a fragment that I had been holding onto. I climbed into the underneath to seek shelter, finding some things to make my sleep comfortable. When you came down and saw me, I got scared. I found a big stick nearby, swinging it at you so you would not come near, or hurt me. Do what with me as you will."

The creature knelt down before Seth, putting his head on the floorboards. Seth did not know what to do, but accept the creature's apology.

"It is OK. I am not hurt too bad, and my sister is taking care of me. You can stand up, and, if you do not mind, could you help us understand how you got here? From where did you come?" Seth realised that with the way Thomasina was treating the shadow, that he would do the same. Maybe this queer looking creature could help them in their quest.

"Rise our new friend. You can help us with our quest, if you can. By what name do you go by?" Bernis asked the creature as his head rose slowly up to face everyone there.

"I do not have a name sir. We are always referred to what level, as mine is shadow of the fifth form. We of the fifth form help the Waddis with the computers and machines that need to be kept running. Without the machines, no one would be able to breathe in home world. Myself, I, would usually assist with the reclaiming of the fragments of the wormholes. That is how I ended in your ship. We were remanufacturing the thread length of a fragment that had been found on earth seven. I started to service it when the trouble happened. The fragment was highly combustible. As soon as we began to work on it, it started to unravel. Some of its threads rolled all over me, making it impossible to escape. It whipped here and there, finally ending up dumping me into your ship. Where the threads went I do not know. All I could see as I fell was a tangle of forms jumping back into the sky above. It may come down, but that would take time."

Thomasina brought the shadow a cup of tea, hoping he would know what it is. He took it from her, bowed very low, and began to drink it. Indeed, this was strange compared to many things.

Bernis stood up, "Please listen to me, everyone. This shadow of the fifth form needs a name. He can be very helpful to us in finding out about the fragment that is maybe human made. This fragment leads from the prisons in the home world to the mines on earth seven in the mountain of Challaque. So, I propose that his name be forever Henry. Everyone needs a name, not a data title. Does everyone agree?" He turned his head to each and every person, including Henry, former shadow of the fifth form. Even Henry, still sipping his tea, was happy.

"May I offer one change?" Henry asked as all were looking, "may I have a last name, like a human? Can I pick this name?"

Everyone agreed.

"From now on my full name will be Henry Shadow. I am a free person of interest to all of you, and I will help you solve this mystery so we can all be free from oppression!"

The now newly named person, as we shall call him, was full of ideas of how to help his new friends. Oddly enough, with his release, his wrinkles on his face began to fade.

"Come everyone! We will eat lunch on deck, now that Tulli is with us!" Thomasina shouted as Titan was circling the boat with the little dog on his back, ready to land. As soon as the Largess gander goose tipped his toes on the deck, the little dog jumped into Bernis' arms, licking his face full of joy. He took the little dog over to Raven, to where he could kiss his mistress in forgiveness. Indeed, he was happy to be with those he loved.

Henry, who had never seen a dog, slowly walked over to where Tulli was, basking in his mistress' arms.

"May I touch the animal? I have never seen one of these before, but I have heard of them from the humans that helped me on the machines. They are called dogs, right?" His hand was hovering over Tulli's head, and, as it was, the dog licked his hand which made Henry giggle.

Raven looked up at Henry, handing a wiggly Tulli over to him. The little dog snuggled into Henry's arms, licking his hands. He bent his head down to see the little dog better. As he did, Tulli began to lick him on the face. It was clear that Tulli liked Henry Shadow. Mr. Shadow certainly liked him, because he smoothed the dog's fur, and as he did, he gained even more kisses. Finally, he handed the dog back to his mistress. Tulli would have none of it, he leaped into Bernis' arms, then to his lap, as he was sitting down beside Titan. Thomasina was serving lunch.

She beckoned Thomas and Henry to join them. They sat together on the other side of Titan.

"I have seen this Largess goose before. The Waddis created him in the lab from a man that had been convicted of traitorous acts. Oh, but that was long ago, probably before any of you here were born, except for you Thomasina."

Thomasina stopped in front of both of them, handing their lunch, as she thought of a way to learn more about this gander.

"How do the two of you know so much about Titan?" Thomasina finally blurted out her questioning verve, "if we survive this what we are going into. All of us will have a discussion about Titan. I found him clinging to a fragment thread that used to be in back of my house. When I got him, he was no more than a gosling. How could a grown man be changed into a gosling?

It does not make any sense to me," she walked off to get more lunch from the galley.

Henry was thoughtful, "Do you think we should explain it to her how he became what he is?" He asked as he picked at the bread on his sandwich with one hand, touching Titan's wing with the other hand.

Thomasina shook her head in a negatory vein, "No, Henry, it would take too long now to explain. For now she must take it for what it is worth. The understanding will come later. Which ever of us survives, or even if the both of us survive. We must sit her down and explain all the process from beginning to end. Then she will understand," she then took a very large bite out of her sandwich. As Henry saw this, he did the same.

Titan was busy eating the nice layout of fruits and vegetables Thomasina had made for him, waggling the whole time. The waggle was no more than a whisper, but he was happy with being back among those he loved dearly, no matter what the past might tell.

Chapter Five

As Raven and Thomasina picked up the lunch dishes, Seth and Bernis had determined that they had finally made it to the coordinates of where the boat was moored when Seth and his sister discovered the initial viewing of the half men. Bernis could feel the coordinates in his bones. Thomasina and Henry shook as their Waddis' cores told them that there was a route to the home world near. It made them sick, they had begun to vomit over the side of the ship. The darkness was still there, waiting. As it received both Henry and Thomasina's vomit, it had proof of the wandering shadow (Henry), and the once man (Thomas). Eagerly the information flowed into the dimension of the home world, letting those listening to it that they were near to recovering at least two outlaws they were seeking. The information was passed to the battery sergeants, who had once been human, turned by the very Waddis that had captured them as children. As far as he was concerned, Seth wanted to do more survey on the darkness that surrounded them in the usually clear blue sea. He knew something was going on, when he watched the two newcomers vomit off the side of the boat. He noticed how the darkness grouped itself around the vomit, as if it was analysing it, somehow. Deep within himself, now that he knew of his sister's and his connection to the Waddis, he felt drawn to the mystery itself. He knew, that now, in home world, they knew of at least Thomas and Henry's position in the scheme of things. In other words, he felt that their position was now known. It was time to speak with Bernis, Thomas, and Henry on the importance of what they had to do. The women would be left without, because where they had to go and do was extremely dangerous. If Thomasina and Raven, with Tulli, of course, had to leave, Titan would get them to safety.

Ultimately this would only be used as a last resort, because both women knew how to treat any sort of wound or sickness. The elder lady made sure that she took enough herbs and healing roots for just that purpose. Everyone was on edge.

Seth got the men together to talk about their next move. he wanted to know, in depth, what Henry and Thomas knew of secret, undercover things in home world and how they were handled. When he told them of his idea about the darkness, Henry spoke up.

"I know there was a network spoken about at home world just before I was taken away. There was much discussion between the humans that helped me work on the machines that they knew of a biological way to get information and positions. Since all of us, including the Waddis are carbon based life forms, there could be a way of detection in the biological sense. It could gather sensitive information by clinging to the very nerves of any being. Positioning could be found out by the biological agent analysing traces of food, excrement, even vomit. Oh my, I think we might have signaled the Waddis where we are. Both Thomas and I got sick earlier and threw up over the railing into the ocean without any thought. I am sorry, my friends, but home world may already know where we are," Henry said, pointing to himself and Thomas.

"This could be very true, my friends. There are humans that were taken from their families at a very young age. They would be raised by the Waddis collective, giving them anything they wanted, in return for learning how to shoot and kill, stalk, chase after beings of their own race. All the while, living, breathing, thinking like a sergeant at arms or such of the order of the High Waddis.

I have seen how they treat their own kind, and it is terrible. If they have detected someone that they are looking for, coming from here. They will send their highest crack troops, all humans, who have been sculpted, some from birth, to the will of the Waddis. These are the most dangerous. Even some of the Waddis are afraid of them. Seth, we need to move the boat to a further location, at least for now," Bernis continued to walk back and forth as he finished.

"I agree with you, Bernis. Let us move about ten miles west. We will still be in the line of the fragment. While we are doing that, I am going to give Titan little sacks of Thomas and Henry's identities. We will need five each from you all. Either spit, cut a bit of your hair, any kind of excreta that you can do. Titan will take it up, dropping them far from here, to throw them off our trail. For now, the fact that Bernis and I are here along with the women, must be held secret. I need you both to create this "bait" right now in these little bags I use for bait fish. They are porous, so do not piss in them. When you are ready, come and get me. I will be telling Thomasina what and where to instruct Titan. It is imperative that this takes no more than a few minutes. The sooner we can leave this position, the better." Seth said and signalled to Titan to be ready to fly. The Largess gander goose began to softly waggle to himself. He was already afraid.

Raven and Thomasina rushed getting through the cleaning of the galley. Hardly a word was said between the two of them. When they saw that they were done, both of the women looked at one another with tears streaming down their cheeks.

"Oh, my precious girl, I am so afraid for you and your brother. I have lived a long and healthy life, you and

Seth have barely started. If it comes to choose who shall go first, it will be me. I can not bear witness to your death, it makes me so sad," Thomasina broke into heaving sobs, clutching Raven close to her. The only girl child of her beloved brother.

Raven stood up, looking at the elder lady in the eyes, "Aunt, oh you are beloved as well. If there comes a time when we have to leave this earth, we will do it together. I will not leave you alone with the burden for all of us. Have a heart, maybe, just maybe, it will not be as bad as we believe. If we hold the truth within our hearts, only good will come for us. Look at the signet ring I wear around my neck. Somehow, in my core, the Waddis legacy may live. When they see this ring, they will drop to their knees, because of Martiz. Some Waddis live to a great age. What if her father still lives? I believe that something connects me with him."

She hugged her aunt tightly, trying to believe her own words that she had just spoken. She believed them, but who else would?

Seth came into the galley, holding both of the women in his arms, "Raven, we are going to move the boat. Thomasina, I need you to speak to Titan, we will need him to do a fly around. I will explain it as we walk to the deck."

Taking both of their hands, the three of them walked through the open door to the deck of the boat.

Bernis knew that he must help all he can. A growing fear was finding itself within his heart. It was not the fear of death, oh no. To his family, he had died many years ago, fighting against the Waddis on the open plains of Tereq. The only and most fear he had was to fail to help his friends both here and on the Waddis home world. He was having a crisis of faith so large that it might make him unable to fight. He felt that he must speak to Raven, before anything else happened. He caught up to her as she was walking back to man the rudder, Seth and Thomasina were in deep discussion over what was needed of Titan.

"Raven, my lady, may I walk with you? There are some things preying on my soul that puts forth the need to speak to you. I hope you do not mind."

As they turned to the angle where the rudder sat, she turned around, facing him.

"You can speak to me about anything you need. My attention is yours to grasp, Bernis."

Raven's liquid black eyes burned with an inner fire. Her cheeks were still wet from crying. Bernis took his large hand, gently wiping her tears, which made her even more sad.

"Dear lady, do not cry. I know you are brave. Whatever there is to do, I know you will do it. I know we have not known each other long. To me, it feels like we have, because I can speak to you about anything, and you will listen. I pray that I do not fail you and everyone else. Most of all, I want to keep you safe. That might sound selfish, but that is how I feel. Please keep me in your heart if times render us from each other."

The big man's face was flush with emotion. A single tear fell from his eye. As it flowed down his cheek, Raven wiped it with her hand. He took that hand tenderly into his, kissing her on the lips as Titan flew over them, shadowing their embrace.

Bernis looked into Raven's dark eyes. He knew that there was a kind soul within. When she looked into his eyes, she knew that fate had met her full of grace.

He kissed her on the cheek as he turned to leave and help Seth. His hand glided over hers, making her breath stop for a moment.

"Be safe in whatever you do, Bernis," she said as he walked away.

"And to you the same, my lady," Bernis said as he walked away.

Oh, how her heart hurt within to see him go. She wanted to keep him safe within her grasp. Hot, steaming tears of fear and anger welled up in her eyes, evaporating in the soft breeze that blew the boat away from its position.

Seth had seen the exchange between his sister and Bernis. All he could think of was that she be happy with what she chooses. In the matters of the heart, he could only act as her confessor. The only time he would step in would be when something physical could happen. His only wish was that the both of them would be happy, up on the upper Piedmont.

Thomas and Henry did not know much of boats and sailing. They were both determined to help out in any way they could. Bernis took them under his wing, showing them how it was done. They wanted to show that they were as much with the group like anyone else. Bernis could see why the Waddis had slaves to do their work. Physically, the two men were useless. In the determination that they showed, however, made up for what they could not do physically. You could say that the two of them could do the work of one man, and that is how he would use them, together.

Seth decided to try something and spoke, "OK, Henry, you can hold this rope. Now hold it as taut as you can, not letting it buckle. Thomas, you take ahold of the end of this rope.

Hold it taut, do not let it buckle. Until I tell you to put the ends that each of you hold into this crook, you can not let go of the rope that you have."

Neither man realised that they were both furling one sail, which Seth and Bernis could do on their own. Walking over to Bernis where both of them could handle the most difficult sails.

Tulli woke up from his nap in the galley. Thomasina was not there. Neither was Raven. He decided to look for his mistress, so he could sit with her. When he entered the deck of the boat, he saw Raven at her post, the rudder.

Immediately he ran to her, jumping into her arms. He snuggled his face all over her shirt, which caused her to giggle. She loved the little dog, and was grateful for his presence. She took him to her seat, putting him on her lap, while she tended the rudder.

Titan flew over her, waggling, to

announce his coming back to the boat. Seth asked Thomasina to check Titan, making sure he had disposed of all the bags of evidence. As she checked him, the gander goose waggled to himself in a tone so low, you could only hear it when you were close to him. The elder lady patted the great head of the gander, noticing that there was something different about him. Instead of his solid brown eyes, he had a black pupil, and an iris of green, surrounded by white, much like a human's eye. Thomas and Henry saw it too. They were done helping with the sails, so they hooked their ropes together, as they were told, walking over to where Titan was. His great eyes looked at them with clarity and spark.

Thomas pointed at the gander's eyes and said, "Look, my lady, your goose, the eyes have changed. This only can happen when they go to their former self. Starvation took the human out of me.

The goose knows exactly what we are doing, and is prepared to help."

He climbed onto a barrel beside the gander to see his eyes better. With his mouth agape with surprise, he also noticed that there were human like eyelashes on each eye. Thomasina came over with a small mirror.

"Before you say anything else, you need to look at yourself," Thomasina said as she handed him the mirror. The pock marked face of a Waddis was slowly disappearing, and his eyes did not bulge out any more. Was he going back to his changed self? Taking the mirror, he faced it at Titan. The gander looked at himself, much like a human would. Why was this happening now?

There could only be one solution, Raven thought to herself. We are so near the fragment of the Waddis, that everything is turning itself around. Why didn't Henry change? All the others were.

Henry could not change, for he was born exactly as you see him. There is only one thing Henry does not know. In order to service the data and machines of the Waddis, the shadows had to work with humans to comprehend what was going on. What Henry did not know was that all shadows were the descendants of a Waddis father and a very short human mother. The babies that were born of normal height were sent to the mines when they got big enough. Some were even groomed as the military guard. The babies that came out as their mother's were sent to work as shadows for the good of the data of the Waddis empire. It was a complicated issue. Hard for any human with common decency to understand. What made it far worse was that some of the children that came out as their mother's were used for an intense breeding project, to make the population of shadows expand. These mothers were always bred with a human.

So, depending on how many generations there were, the Waddis influence was fluctuating. In the very DNA of the subjects, the Waddis influence waned. Home world becoming something else?

Raven was right in how she thought, but she did not know all of the information that went into the understanding of the whole situation. She would have to see Henry for what he was, just Henry.

Seth and Bernis guided the boat to a further place, so they could observe what the darkness did when it came in contact with the bags Titan had seeded into the ocean. They had dropped anchor, but when they looked over the side, the darkness had left. When they looked to where the bags had been seeded, the darkness could be seen, going from position to position. It was doing just as they had thought.

Seth decided to move the boat yet again, staying on the diagonal of the fragment, but going further from their previous position. He wanted to confuse this secret gathering chemical, whatever it was. The very movement of the darkness told him that the intelligence within it was artificial, manufactured by the shadows and whatever humans were in the data labs of the Waddis. This could also be its Achilles' heel. A broken part of a community tearing itself apart with inbreeding, slaves running the machines, and who know what else was going on in home world. He motioned Henry to come over to him. As a priority they were keeping their voices down because of what was going on. He knew Henry could read. He caught him reading off of the side of a box as clear as any human. he decided to have Henry write his answers, because of the high volume of his voice.

"Here Henry, I want you to write your answers to me on this piece of paper. Here is a pencil to use. When I ask a question, just write the answer down on this piece of paper. After we are done, we shall read it together. Understand?"

Henry nodded his head in answer to the question, he only knew too well how loud his voice could get.

"OK, we'll start with this one. Were you brought up by your parents, or were you in a home, where many of your kind lived. Was your mother or father human? How were you trained? Who was your teacher? Was your teacher human or Waddis? Did you create any programs within the data stream on your own? Is the darkness the only biological type of seeking mechanism? What do you know of the diagonal of the fragment and the half men?" Seth patiently waited for the answers.

Henry was trying to write as fast as he could. He even began to cry, because of all the emotional stress it was putting on him. Seth said he could stop, but the little man insisted to finish what he had started. Finally, he had finished answering the questions Seth put forth to him. The first question was if his mother or father had been human? He answered carefully in his childish print, "I only ever knew my mother. We lived in a brood house off of the main square in home world. I do not know what a brood house is, but that is what it was called. When I got older, and was able to work, we moved to a small house outside of main city in home world. I had to live close to where I worked, because I had to walk both ways. Anyway, to the best of my knowledge, my mother was half human. She was much shorter than I was then. She is now deceased, and I still live in the little house given to us."

The second question was about how he was trained. He answered thusly, "I was trained from the age of ten to service the data machines under the close watch of a human trainer. He was very good to me, and helped me learn, any things. But there was one day that he never came back. I asked about him, but no answer was given. Waddis high council teamed me with a shadow who was mostly human. I had to listen carefully to him, because if I asked a question about anything he had previously said, he would hit me hard with a thick bar he kept close to him. I was glad when they moved him to another machine room, and I began to work on my own. By then I knew all of what had to be done about the data. I even helped to train some humans to help me in the room I worked in."

The third question was answered by the second response. So this continues to the fourth question about creating any programs. Henry seemed to have pause with this question, because he wrote that he did not know how to answer it. He did innovate some of the programs, but the main work was carried out by the human workers.

The fourth question about the darkness and biological seeking mechanism was a bit sketchy. He indicated that the programs like that were handled by an elite group of programmers that he did not work with. That kind of thing was kept in deep secret. The ones that worked on it were not allowed to leave the room they worked in, so they would have no problem of knowledge leaking out to the general public in home world. But, he did hear some humans that were working in his room, speaking about a friend of theirs that had been assigned to that room. The only time that they saw him after that was when they were bringing what remained of his body out of the room. To them,it looked like that he had been eaten.

The fifth question was clearly the most important, about the diagonal of the fragment, of which the boat was in direct contact with. Henry was clearly excited about this question. He indicated that he had helped to build the fragment that would travel from the home world to the mines on earth seven and the mountains of Challaque. This very same causeway took the half men back to the home world after their time in the mines. In fact,that was how he got tangled with a fragment of the very same, sending him into the boat where they found him. Again, he apologised for his actions when he came into contact with Seth.

"OK. So with a fragment of a fragment, you can be sent anywhere with no direction? Is it possible to only send and not have the capability of coming back? Bernis, I need you to check the star charts, and see if this is possible. Henry, how would you get a fragment of a fragment?" Seth reached out his hand to the little man, motioning for him to write his answer down.

Henry wrote, "You do not need much to divide the filaments of the fragment. Think of a string in a tangle. To get it out of the tangle, just retrace its route, coming back with one string. The same can be done to a fragment. All you need is a very sharp knife, and the will to do it. Funny thing about fragments. They can feel the negative energy emanating from a body. If it senses the negative, it closes its fibers so tightly that nothing could render them apart. I would be glad to do that when the fragment appears tonight. I have been handling these things nearly my whole life. Tell me how many fibers you need,and it shall be done,my friend," Henry held his answer in his hand, proudly giving it to Seth.

"Awesome, my friend! Let us take ten threads from the fragment, and, as an experiment, send ten Waddis, or even human to a place they are not familiar with. If we have success tonight, we can take it entirely apart by tomorrow. Is that copacetic with you, Henry? Can we keep the threads for another time?" Seth was pacing as he was speaking what ever flowed from his mind.

Henry shook his head and answered, "I do not know if that is possible without a frozen zone. The threads are active for about three weeks after their separation. But, they must be frozen until they are used, otherwise the energy flow from the threads dissipates, and they are unusable."

Bernis' eyes lit up and he said, "By all that is holy! We have the storage box for the fish. Does it not freeze the fish as soon as they are put into the box? We could use that to store the excess threads, if we need to."

Seth looked at everyone and said, "Depending on what we can do with all this new found information. I would say we have a leg into the so called home world and the freeing of its slaves and any other being or creatures that work for the greater good of only the Waddis empire. We even know that there might be an upsurge of home world Waddis rebelling against the old order. We need to iron out a plan on what to do, as soon as it is three minutes past twelve. The fragment will not be in the boat, but along side it. I believe that this might be a better way to, at least, observe the coming and going of the miners and their guards. Henry, if you can gain us ten filaments of the fragment, we will store them in the cold box until we are totally ready to engage our plan. Tonight is observation only. Quiet from now on it the utmost of importance."

Henry handed Seth a slip of paper. He had thought very carefully what to put on the paper. It read, "Seth, I have one question for you, and then I will be done. When we are done with this caper, can I go to my old house on home world and retrieve something that is important to me? I will go by myself, and return with what I need to get, by myself. Thank you." He blushed rose red as Seth read it.

"My friend, if we come out of this alive and kicking, I will allow you to do just that. You deserve the happiness that has been taken away from you. I promise you that."

Seth reached out to Henry, patting him on the shoulder. He took note of the blush on Henry's face. *"Waddis could not do that. This guy has a lot of human in him,"* he thought to himself.

Now it was time to plan for tonight. Henry was to procure the filaments needed from the fragment after the miners and their guards have passed. He would have a window of about two minutes. This strategy would enable them to take the filaments, while no one from home world would know of any penetration of the manufactured fragment. Henry hoped to be able to examine the filaments in their frozen state. There would be no danger of removal to another place while the filaments were in the frozen state.

Bernis thought that it would be a good idea to tie a string onto Henry's waist, so they could keep tabs on him, reeling him in when the time had passed. Everyone seemed to like that idea, because it was simple and did not require any instruments. Henry was excited about his role in this first try. Maybe it would make everyone trust him more as he worked with them. Most of all he hoped that they would let him go back to his little house to save one thing that he truly missed.

He could live the rest of his life alone, if
he were let to do this. The whole feeling
of it warmed his heart.

Thomasina called everyone to eat
dinner on top deck. The breezes had been
good, but within the galley it was very
hot. The elder lady needed a little break.
Before calling for dinnertime, she decided
to pay a visit to where Raven was. When
she got there, she found Raven looking
ahead with Tulli comfortably asleep in
her lap and said, "Raven, tie up the
rudder and help me dish out dinner. OK?
I could use the help, love."

Raven looked up at her beloved
aunt and smiled. Securing Tulli in her
arms, she took the rudder up, tying it to
the side. Tulli was small enough to sit
underneath her arm as she did this. He
did not mind at all, licking her arm as she
tried to finish her job. Thomasina took
Tulli in her arms, so Raven could finish.
Soon, both the ladies were on their way to

the galley. Soon, everyone was sitting in a tight circle on deck. Titan was softly waggling to himself, despite the fact that his eyes looked totally human. Thomasina had fed him as soon as he got back from his trek, so he was now full, and peacefully napping. Tulli snuggled into one of his great wings, trying to get out of a soft wind that had turned cold.

Bernis had managed to sit by Raven. He was still very shy, but by a little bit Raven brought him out of his shell. The both of the blushed when they spoke to one another. Thomasina nodded at them, happy that they had found each other. She prayed that they would survive this thing they were all tangled in. If only, she wished in her heart. If only.

Thomas was continuing to change to being human. The more he ate, the more he changed. He soon would be back to his old state before he had gone to the mines.

"If only Ruby could come back with all this. I would truly love to be with her again. Maybe just see her and hug her, telling Ruby how much I truly loved her."

When Thomasina and Raven began to pick up the last of dinner, the younger of them noticed something in the water. Raven was dumb struck as she wailed out her brother's name, "Seth, come quick! Something is happening in the water over the bow!" She handed her dishes to Henry, who was glad to be of help to the elder lady. But he also wanted to see what was causing Raven to be so excited. Thomasina put her pots down on the deck, she instructed Henry to do the same. She took him by the hand, leading him to where everyone else was.

Seth leaned over the bow as far as he could go. Raven was huddling within Bernis' arms, the both of them looking

awestruck at what they were seeing.
Henry kept his hand holding
Thomasina's. None of them really knew
the impact of what they were looking at.

As far as the eye could see, there
was no darkness any more. For some
reason, it had fled. What replaced it was a
whole ocean full of dead bodies, human
and Waddis. Bernis was able to see some
of the miners he had worked with. Above
all of this was a very large fragment that
was coming unhinged. Filaments from
the fragment were slapping everywhere.
When the filament touched a body, it
would disappear, only to reappear a mile
or two away. This was a dangerous
situation. The boat had to be moved away
from this horrible death toll. They would
be next if they did not back away soon.

Raven ran to the rudder for her
brother to tell her where to move. Tulli
went with Thomasina in the galley, while
Henry helped her with the dinner dishes.
As soon as they were done, he gave the

elder lady a hug, heading for the door to the top deck. As he left, he patted Tulli's head, and the dog licked him on his hand. He felt that he needed to do this, so the little animal wouldn't worry about them. Walking upon the deck, he could see the sails were full. Bernis and Seth were manning the sails, and throttling the wheel to get them further away. He saw what was needed to be done. A stray filament was heading towards the boat. He took out his flensing knife, ready to cut the filament if it came too close.

Thomas was helping with the sails. Since he started to go back to his human self, strength had returned to his body. He was glad to help. "I will do this for you, my blessed Ruby!" He yelled into the wind as he took hold of the ropes, setting the sail so they could move away from where they were.

Henry saw the filament directly overhead. He climbed up the main mast with his flensing knife ready. He knew to not touch the end of the filament, so he grabbed the string as it made its way past him. With his hands, he caught ahold of the filament, cutting enough from it so it would not touch the ship or anyone in it. Quickly, he wound the filament piece into a ball, tying it with string, so it would not come apart. He then secured it into a cotton pouch he kept with him. The filament would hold there until they could store it in the cold box. Swiftly, he climbed down the main mast to see if there was anything else he could do.

Seth saw and wondered what Henry did. He was standing at the bottom of the main mast when Henry came down.

"I am glad that you are with us. But, I do hope that you secured the filament that was left hanging," he said, pointing to the filament string, now hanging, quite limp, in the air.

It was still attached to the fragment that had literally belched all the life out of it across the ocean beyond them now.

Henry took out his flensing knife, holding it up for Seth to see, "I know what I am doing, my friend. My flensing knife burns the end of the filament rendering it useless until I open it again with the opposite end of the same knife. I took as much filament as I could, rolling it up and tying it with string. You see this cotton pouch? Well, for now; the filament rests in there. I have ten hours to get it to freezing. I am here to help, Seth, with everyone. Our very lives demands that we keep our heads together,not to lash out at one another. The filament is part of the fragment. There can be communication between them as far as negative energy is concerned. We must be as positive as possible," he said as he folded his knife carefully, putting it into his pocket.

"I am sorry, Henry. For a moment my worst fears came to a head. I felt anxious about what was happening, and did not understand what you were doing. Please accept my firmest apology," Seth put his hand out for Henry to shake. Immediately Henry grasped Seth's hand within both of his, letting him know all was good between them.

"Come Seth, let us see what is happening. We can work on this together."

Henry and Seth walked towards the bow where everyone else was gazing at the devastation that greeted them.

Thomasina thought to herself, *"The holocaust has come back to greet me again. This time it has included everyone, the victims, the conqueror, the conquered. I thought all this was past. Because we did not learn from the last one, when I was a child, I am doomed to see it again. This one has been caused by the oppressors that gave no quarter.*

By the law that we live and breathe! I am lost in the enormity and sadness of it." She bowed her head to pray, not noticing that Raven and Bernis were standing beside her. Each of them took a side, sweeping her into their arms. All were praying now.

Henry looked out to the distancing ocean. As far as he could see there were bodies. All kinds of bodies. Waddis, human, humanoids, the brooders, everyone that lived in home world was represented in the deep blue water. The darkness had fractured itself. Breaking loose of those who controlled it. Going off on its own to die. Ashes to ashes, dust to dust. The manufactured fragment had exploded and killed all who were in it, and near it. He had to think to see what he could do. So, he sat on a fat coil of rope and closed his eyes. As Henry sat there, deep in thought, the others were too busy accounting for all the dead that they were seeing, stretching for miles from the boat.

The fragment had also ended its life. It was created for a purpose, to transport people, beings from point A to point B. Something had happened to end the fragment. There were no more filaments wildly arcing over the ocean, dropping bodies here and there. The whole system had died, filaments and all, along with its possible creators.

Chapter Six

In the midst of all the terror and chaos, henry had reached a calm. He could see the little house he and his mother shared. He could also see his little cat, Fannie. Some how when he was working on a tanglement in the main fragment, she had become ensnared within it. She did not meow or make any such other cat noise, she peeped. Opening her mouth by the smallest bit, she peeped while her long whiskers would sweep back and forth with the motion of the peep. He put her in a box he had his lunch in, keeping her there until it was time to go home. No checkpoints for him. The humans were the only ones checked, because they were always trying to escape. He brought Fannie home to his mother, letting her open the box where the little gold kitten greeted her with a peep. She loved her large brown eyes, how they followed movement. She also liked to watch her hunt for mice. When she found one, she would play with it for a while, even throwing it into the air once or twice. When it was firmly terrorised, she would kill it, deftly cutting it to pieces with her claws. She would always bring the tiny heart to his mother. Kind of like a thank you for being with her. Letting her sleep in her bed with her at night. It went on this way until his mother passed. When Henry had finished the grave, he was patting the soil on it so he could plant one of his mother's favorite flowers on her grave. It would be good to mark it, he thought. Fannie thought otherwise.

One day he saw Fannie burying something on the top of the grave. He waited while she wandered to the house to rest. As he dug at the spot, he saw it. It was a mouse heart, just like Fannie would give his mother when she was alive. He had some seeds in his pocket, random seeds from here and there. He planted all of them on top of the heart, patting it down with extra soil, so Fannie would not dig it up.

Henry wanted to go back, one last time, to check on the grave, and to try to find Fannie, so he could take her with him. There was plenty of food there,plus a small brook in the back of the house. So she would not want for food and drink. But, he felt that need to go and get her, so she could be with him. He needed her for his existence. He would ask Seth if he could go on a trek to see what had happened within home world. How whatever they were now seeing had affected the whole dimension. Finally, he opened his eyes. Seth was standing right in front of him.

"Ah, sleeping Henry? You have been in this repose for at least an hour. It's OK. Nothing has changed in the ocean, except we are seeing multiple fins in the water, and bodies are beginning to disappear. Ridge sharks, I think. Those monsters can smell blood from miles away. Oh well, at least the ocean is getting a clean up. Any thoughts?"

Seth continued to pace back and forth in front of Henry. It did not bother him. He felt sorry for Seth, so far away from his emotions.

Henry thought a minute, pursing his lips like he did when the thoughts were so intense, he had to calm them down.

"You know the fragment is dead. The filaments connected to it are dead as well. Some kind of devastation has happened in home world, otherwise you would see the High Guard making their sweeps. I think, even so, that something has happened to the very dynamic of the Waddis. I have this filament in my pouch. I can use it to go to home world. When I am there, I will see what truly happened to the dimension. If you and Bernis wish to go, come along. This filament is big enough for the three of us. All I have to do is to use my flensing knife on it again, to re-engage it to move us.

But, we must be careful, not separating, because that might mean that one of us could be left within the dimension. Think about it. Talk to Bernis about it. We will get together and be a team?" Henry said as he shielded his eyes from the noonday sun. It seemed to shine much harsher than before.

Thomas opted to stay with the women, just in case. Titan was back to his Largess gander goose self. His human eyes were replaced by his gander eyes. He seemed not so upset any more. Tulli stayed in Raven's arms. He did not want to leave her for even a moment.. Some bodies were still floating about the ocean. It seemed like the ridged sharks had left. Curiously enough, the only things that the sharks ate was the human dead. Not a single dead Waddis was touched. Their bodies began to swell under the hot sun. Some, further away had swelled up so hard that they had burst.

Not a lovely sight to see after all that happened.

Seth walked over to Raven, "Sister, I know you are a crack shot with my old rifle. Pick off the dead floaters. Shoot each one once in the abdomen, so they can expand and sink. Don't shoot any near the boat. We don't want guts all over the side of the boat. Can you do this while we go into home world to see what we can find?"

Raven looked up at her brother, hugging Tulli even closer. She did not want to tell her brother that she was afraid for him. Actually, afraid for all of them. What if this was a giant trap? They would not know unless it happened.

"Yes, Seth, I will do that. Do we have enough ammo? I will go look at the supply hold before I do anything like that," Raven using that as an excuse to go somewhere by herself so she could cry. She did not like to shed tears in public.

Seth went over to the galley to talk to Thomasina. He also had to drop Tulli off with her, so Raven could look for the ammo, and the old rifle. Bernis saw her go down, so he quietly followed her. When he got there, he saw her at the bottom of the stairs, wiping her eyes. He tapped her, gently, on the shoulder. Her glistening black eyes looked at this man. This man she might never see again. She turned to him, putting her arms around his neck. She kissed him full on the lips.

"I will be waiting for you here when you all get back," Raven reached up to kiss him again.

Bernis took her face into his hands, kissed both of her eyes, then leaned in to give her a kiss she would remember, "I will be back, my beautiful lady. You can be assured of that." They both kissed each other one more time. Bernis heard Seth calling for him. Turning to leave, he kissed her again, "Do not forget me, my lovely." He then ran up the stairs to go with Seth and Henry.

Raven dried her face with the arm of her shirt. "Be safe, my loves. All of you, come back to those who wait," Heavily sighing, she turned around to look for the extra ammo. It happened to be right beside her all the time, in plain sight.

Henry carefully took out the filament he was going to use for them to get into home world. With his flensing knife, he teased one of the ends. Sparks shot out of it, in a circular fashion. He knew that the filament they had was quite alive. The three men had taken a small skiff that Seth always tied to the side of the boat to use in unusual circumstances. They knew the fragment was dead. What Henry was unsure of, was how it would react when he tied the filament onto it. Choosing to be the first one to go into the fragment, he carefully stepped on a part of a piece that was big enough to serve a man. The piece sloped down a bit, but did not touch the water. This was good, because water, especially salt water, would make the fragments come to life. He had seen that happen in the lab once before. It had killed three humans and two Waddis before it was removed. Henry motioned for Seth and Bernis to follow him.

Seth anchored the skiff, he did not want to encounter any ridged sharks. By all around them, he could not see any, but that did not mean they were there.

Henry had learned to quieten his voice, so he started to explain what he was doing, "I am first going to de-flens this end, and attach it to this particularly drooping piece of filament that was poking out over our heads. Now, one of you needs to grab a hold of me, and the other grab ahold of the first. Once that is done, I will de-flens the other end." He could hear a faint crackling in his ears, which made him a little nervous. Seth said in a low voice, "We are ready Henry."

With the knowledge of the ready, he said a short prayer his mother had taught him years ago, "Please, the giver of all life, keep ours safe." He slowly deflensed the open end, after first twisting it around his wrist. The end crackled to life, sending a surge of electrical sparks through the men. They all held as tightly as they could. Henry held even tighter to the filament end as they started to rise and move through the air.

Within moments they were transported to the dimension of home world. Henry did not tell Bernis and Seth one thing. Whoever manipulates the filament within a fragment has control of where they go. Few knew of this, he was one of them. So that his last utmost thoughts were to see his little house and Fannie again, his wish was met.

Many who dealt with these almost mythical contraptions would panic and let their minds wander to things that they hadn't properly considered these, in particular would wind up in desolate and unheard of places, as he did when the filament broke loose within the lab, sending him to the boat. With a shared thud, the men landed on a dirt and rocky road right in front of his house. Henry did not say anything yet, because he had to secure the filament. He used his knife, closing the connection for now. He needed to hide it out of reach and site so that it wouldn't be bothered with. This was their only link back to the reality they had all chosen to live in. Henry decided to tie it on a topmost branch of an old tree that stood on the other side of the road. Shinning up the trunk of the tree, he made it to the top, securing the end so no harm would come to anything or anyone that discovered it. If discovered by a human or Waddis, they would have to know how to "bring it to life," as he did.

Henry jumped down off of a lower branch of the old tree. Many a cool evening he had gone up there as a child, so he could be free and think for a while. His mother always knew where to find him. "Well friends, looks like we landed in a spot I know personally. Welcome to my little home. If you do not mind, I would like to pick up a few things before we go on our trek," he said as he walked across the road to the door of the house, opening it with a latch that was on the front of the door. "Come, follow me," he said as he slowly walked into the house, trying to see if Fannie was there, with out Seth and Bernis noticing.

Henry heard a faint rustle within the green grass that surrounded the house. Directly in front of him was his mother's grave, now covered with little shoots and tubers in abundance, it made him smile to see this, always keeping it within his heart of memory. Again, he heard the rustling around him, this time more determined. Whispering the name, "Fannie," he kneeled in the grass. Seth and Bernis were behind Henry now, wondering if he was praying, or something else.

Turning around to face his friends, they could see that his eyes were welled with tears. He held up his hands so they could see the small cat with the gentle brown eyes, now staring at them. She let out a slight, "Peep," as if greeting them. Bernis turned his fingers inward, letting the small creature bump his hand with her head, peeping very softly. Seth looked on this little visa with astonishment. He thought that the cat had died out centuries ago on all the earths. A virulent plague had decimated the cat populations, therefore increasing the mouse and rat populations.

On some earths, they had to import Possums, so the rodent population could be kept down. Reaching out, he stroked the cat's soft fur. She turned to look at him, peeping very softly.

"This is what I came for. May I introduce Fannie. She has been with me a good while, and she is a good mouser. If it is OK, I would like to take her with us. She can go into my backpack. I used to sneak her into work that way, to keep her safe with me after my mother passed. If I can not take her, I will stay here and take my chances, after helping you both find out if there is any Waddis threat or not," Henry said and curled his arms around the little cat, as she peeped and settled herself within his arms.

Seth and Bernis looked at one another. They both knew that Henry was needed with them in this dimension and on earth nine. Being of only one thought, they both put out their hands for Henry to shake, forgetting that he was holding Fannie. Bernis gladly took Fannie in his arms, reaching out with his free hand to shake Henry's hand. Seth shook Henry's other hand, saying, "I guess this means we are a team."

Bernis handed Fannie back to Henry, as she peeped softly, making her whiskers wiggle. He took off his backpack, snuggling her within it. As he put the backpack back on, he could feel the little cat's love for him, as she softly peeped to herself. Soon she was deep in sleep, knowing she was safe now. She had not felt safe while Henry was lost to her. She had lost one friend, she did not want to lose another.

Henry led his friends on a backroad that would lead to the work point, where all the data was stored and the fragments had been attempted. The strangled forest looked gloomy under the dimension's grey sky.

Their eyes were used to it, but they had to be cautious of any shadows around. They were not the same as shadows in the earths. These shadows were disguises for dangerous things and creatures. Perhaps even Waddis.

Raven sat there on the deck, looking out on the ocean. She had already picked off the remaining Waddis bodies that were floating on the surface. She did not have any satisfaction to the ones she hit, sending them immediately down to the ocean bottom. She could see no human bodies left. The ridged sharks had taken care of all of them. She wondered why the sharks did not attack the Waddis bodies. *"Strange,"* she thought to herself, it is almost as if they didn't taste right.

Thomas was now looking very human, less bony now. He sat beside Raven, scanning the horizon for anything unusual. Somehow he felt that there would be another upsurge of anything

Waddisian. He really did not know for sure. He continued to gaze outward.

"Thomas, when we were in the cairn, Martiz wrote that the only way to kill a Waddis was through trauma to their heads. Is that true? If that is so, then why were all the Waddis found floating dead with other kinds of wounds that killed them?" Raven turned to look at Thomas to make sure he was listening to her.

"My lady, when a Waddis is killed, the central impact must be on the head, especially the top of the head. The ones I saw floating on the ocean looked, to me, as if their heads had exploded from the inside. Did you not notice how big their heads were? They were all swollen from the impact of whatever made that fragment implode. It could have been sabotage. All of them, human and Waddis were dead before they hit the water. I think you missed one," Thomas said as he pointed starboard to a Waddis body bumping against the ship. Raven got her rifle ready to shoot as they looked over the side. There it was. The Waddis' head was twice its normal size. Thomas had been right. She took aim at the body. When the bullet hit it, a loud hissing sound emanated from the Waddis. Within seconds the body sank quickly into the murky depths. She looked at Thomas, watching the body dive bomb itself down to the ocean floor.

"Thomas, don't Waddis have any guts?"

"Not much, my lady. They are mostly brains and skin. That's what I looked like when you rescued me from the water. I do thank you for that. As long as my diet is good, I will continue to be human, even aging as humans do," Thomas replied, raising his hand to pat Raven on the shoulder, turning his gaze back onto the ocean. Raven did the same.

Chapter Seven

The three friends continued to walk through the forest. It was known between all of them that quiet was the order. They wanted to detect whatever was there first before it could detect them. The path through the forest began to wane, turning into a gravel paved walkway. Despite the crooked forms the trees made, this path was neat and well made. Henry was busy writing on a stylus he picked up from his house. It was made of two thin pieces of wood, held together with string. On the inward surface of each plank was a thick coating of unmeltable wax. He would write upon it with a sharpened stick. When he was done, he would simply close the stylus, erasing what was written. Henry wrote fast on the tablet, wanting Bernis and Seth to read it before they reached work point.

"This path was crafted by humans. There was the hope, that if they did a good job, they would be rewarded with their freedom.

This path encircles all the area of work point. Oh yeah, when the humans finished the path, they were executed where they had finished this very same path. The Waddis dumped their bodies in a hole that had been dug the day before by the same humans. They had been led to believe that they were to create a water pool, for fish to swim in. This little story will prepare you for what you might see. Just know that I did not play a part in it. My only duty was to stream the data for the fragments."

He handed the stylus over to Seth so they could read it, stopping while they digested the meaning of it all.

Seth handed the stylus back to Henry, they walked in tighter ranks now. The path was leading them into the heart of the work point. No one really knew what they would find or see. Silent prayers were lent by all of them as they continued to walk towards the grey building up ahead.

Henry stopped dead in his tracks. Not more than ten feet away, dead bodies lined the path coming from the work point. By they way the dead were laying, it looked like they had been thrown about at great speed. The Waddis dead's heads were swollen with trauma. The human bodies looked like something had picked them up, cracking them in two. There was only one thing that could do that, a fragment rupture, much worse than they had seen over the ocean. By the damage to the buildings, the fragment had been larger and more magnified than ones Henry had seen. Extreme caution was the norm now. Silently, the three men clung close to one another, taking even the same step at the same time. Bernis stopped, making the others do the same. About twenty feet away was the gaping maw of a tangled fragment. The filaments were still within the fragment wall. This was worse than what they had already seen.

This fragment could suck them up, and spit them out dead, because of its reckless nature. They had to find a way to approach this behemoth. As they stood there, a young Waddis was running towards them.

"Run, if you can. Run far away. The data stream imploded all the fragments. They are wild and unapproachable. These things can detect you just from your breath!"

As the young Waddis gave the fragment a wide berth, trying to evade it, the thing turned itself, sucking up the Waddis, they could see his body bumping hard on the insides of the beast. Within a few seconds it spit him out, nearly dead on the ground at the three friends' feet.

"All of them have gone rogue. We have signed our death sentence. Try to save yourselves," The young Waddis whispered as he closed his eyes in death.

Henry kneeled down beside the dead Waddis, "Please, with the forces that are around us, let his soul be free, so it can serve in the next kingdom He might have been of a foreign way, but his core was still like us, human though different. Bless him," he put his hand over the dead eyes that had opened after death, the spark to close them gone. Quietly, he stood up, and faced his friends.

"We are in a very dangerous situation here. The fragments are going to suck up all the life they can, spitting it out lifeless. Work point is no more. The data superseded the need, fattening the fragments bent on the destruction of anything and everything. We must go on a different route to the core city. If it is the same there, I suggest we go back to earth nine. Follow me," he said as he turned away from all the bodies and fragments waving up and down in search for living flesh.

Titan woke up from his slumber. He started to waggle loudly, as if to warn anyone around him, that all was not right. Little Tulli ran into Thomasina's galley, seeking her lap for a safer place. She found him, whimpering under Raven's bed. Coaxing him out, she took him in hand to see what Titan was saying.

The largess gander goose was waggling, almost wailing loudly. Thomas and Raven had already come to him to try to help his anguish. Raven could feel that it was for Seth, Bernis, and Henry that he wailed. She began to shake, her eyes turned solid black. As soon as Thomasina saw it she took hold of her, putting Tulli down, so she could get a better grip.

"Raven, walk through the walls that surround us. Find the ones loved and lost so we can help them."

Raven then fainted, Thomas helping to catch her as she fell to the deck. Tulli was yelping in fear, for he could sense the evil, but he did not know where it was.

As Raven fell, her eyes turned into black pools, that no one could see through, except Thomasina. Unknown to both, Titan was already in her subconscious, waiting for her. In the mist of her mind, she rose up from the floor with no help. A thin grey clothed man was standing in front of her, holding out his hand spoke, "Hello,Raven. I am Titan. Or, rather, what used to be Titan. Look to my eyes, and you will see me clearly."

Raven sought out his eyes, finding them a deep and comforting blue-grey. She knew that they were his, because what he was now had the same eyes.

"Hello, Titan. I have often wondered what you would of looked like as a human.

My aunt tells me that she has seen your true self a few times, but does not understand how you changed."

Titan lowered his head, softly shaking it back and forth as he did on earth when he waggled, saying; "the truth is that the Waddis did this to me in one of their experiments. I was a human worker in one of their data labs. They decided to try gene coding, or changing one life for another. What you see on earth nine is the result of that. I still think like a human, that is how Thomasina speaks to me. I love her dearly. But, let us get to the present. Seth, Bernis and Henry are in great trouble. The fragments that the Waddis tried to create have become life sucking worm holes, whose only vice is to kill and kill again. For no reason other than that. Somehow the data got twisted in the making of the fragments from dissected pieces of the worm holes. That was their mistake.

If they would have made one from their own, cleaned data, this would not have happened. Right now, Henry is the only one that can save them."

"So what am I supposed to do? I am not even with them," Raven sobbed as she spoke.

"My child, it is alright. You alone have the capability of your ancestor, Martiz. As she did, so can you. I will lead you through it, so you will know for the next time. Here, take my hand and follow me."

Titan gently took her hand, and walked beside her, softly saying; "Whatever will become, we will do it together, my lady. Love is the biggest trust you can have. I know you love Seth, your brother. I also know you are beginning to love Bernis, as he does you. Come, let us go and save the many earths that surround us, as well as the ones you love so dearly.

The wormholes and their fragments,even the filaments must be taken down. We will need Henry to help us."

Titan and Raven walked slowly through what looked like a doorway, lined with turquoise (for protection). As they were walking under a huge blooming tree, Henry fell down. To anyone else, he looked profoundly asleep. In reality, his conscious was needed to guide Raven and Titan to the very mouths of the worm holes, fragments and filaments. He thought he had woken up from a fall. Ready to help his friends again. But, this was not to be so. In front of him was Raven, whom he knew, and Titan whom he did not. He did know this, however. He was in a place that he had never been, it frightened him to be there.

"Where are Seth and Bernis? I must lead them around home world, so we can find out what has happened to everyone.

The Waddis built fragments have gone rogue. They were built from snippets of the other fragments and older worm holes. It is disastrous! They behave like beasts in the plain. Looking for live bodies they can devour. I must go back to protect my friends!" Henry said, shaking in anger and fear. Something within himself made him calm down. He knew Raven and this other Titan would not harm anyone.

Titan laid a hand on henry's shoulder, "Your body is back in home world. Seth, Bernis, and your body have been absorbed by the giant tree you just passed under. No one will be detected while your mind is here. You remember being told about of the tree of life? Well, this tree that you and your friends are in, is the last one of its kind. After all is said and done in home world, that tree will be one of the remaining. Do not worry, your friends, like yourself are in an incubation mist.

Nothing can harm any of you while within the tree."

Raven looked at Henry. Her eyes were solid black, no whites could be seen. Henry knew of this because he had seen it before in the breeder houses. Their were many Waddis/human combinations. When it was just right, these combinations could see things others couldn't. He did not fear her, for he knew the goodness of her heart, "What do you wish of me to do? How can I help? I have but one question. I want to know how Fannie is taking all of this. She is in a backpack with my body. I do not want any harm to come to her."

Titan's eyebrows shot up, "Oh, the peeper cat? She is fine. I transferred her life form to the boat where the women, Thomas and Tulli reside. She will be there waiting for you when your job is done. Do not worry, Thomasina will know where she is from. She will be in her care.

We must proceed if we can."

An urgent thought came to Henry, "I do not know where all the worm holes, fragments and filaments are. Do we need to find a particular one, or all of them? Bernis has a star map of most of the wormholes, but when I saw it, it didn't look complete. Or could there be a creator worm hole, that lays out the fragments, and filament like insect eggs?"

"Indeed. That might be the case with this. Since they seem to be going rogue, then there must be a spark of life within. All of the transporting that has been done since the wormholes were created, there's got to be a shred or two of a creature's or person's essence within. If they were absorbed by which route they took, then the resemblance will be there. That is all well and good, but we must find the first of all of them. To destroy it would destroy all the others, because they are linked in their innermost core.

Do you know anything of a first one, Henry?" Raven asked as she looked at him with those hypnotic, liquid black eyes.

Thomasina was walking to the galley. She asked Thomas to watch over Raven's body while she was in the "state." The girl must not be moved or touched, because that would break the connection, and all would be lost. As she entered the galley, she saw a small animal in the corner with Tulli. It must not be any trouble, otherwise Tulli would be whimpering. As she stepped closer, she could see what it was, "Why, a peeper cat. I thought they were long gone from the earths. Who has sent you to me sweetheart? Was it Henry? Yes, yes, I suspected so," she picked up the little creature. Fannie peeped softly at her, with her long whiskers quivering, every time she peeped. She put her head to Thomasina's forehead, softly rubbing it back and forth.

"Ah, so your name is Fannie, little girl. Well, you are with us and Tulli now. If you would like to stay with him, I will get both of you a bowl of water and some treats," Thomasina set the little cat next to Tulli, who was wagging his tail at his new friend. She peeped softly at him, rubbing her head on his. The elder lady gave them both a bowl of clear water, and some food on a tiny plate each. Fannie looked up at Thomasina with her large brown eyes, peeping so softly you could barely hear it. Tulli waited patiently for her to start eating, then he ate from his dish.

"You are most welcome miss Fannie. It is a pleasure to meet you. I am glad that you and Tulli are friendly. I must go and take some hot tea and a sandwich to Thomas. He is looking after Raven while she is helping Henry deep within the veil. All things supernatural can happen from there. I will be right back," Thomasina said and took the tea and sandwich out to Thomas, humming under her breath.

Henry started to think hard, knowing that he had heard something of a "primal" wormhole. One so large it could swallow worlds. What he had also heard, he could not prove. This primal worm hole actually produced other worm holes, fragments, and filaments. It was as old as the universe, possibly older. But was there something that controlled it? His memory came into fold. Slowly, he began to remember the story he was told. An elder Waddis was discussing it with another Waddis. The elder one had indicated that this primal worm hole was in blank space. There could be nothing near it, or it would swallow it whole. He also remembered that the elder spoke of a control that stayed with the wormhole. He said that it lived on the upper lip of the worm hole, the job it did was really unknown. Except for this, he had heard the control could actually stop it.

How this control could stop it was unknown to the elder and himself. But, the more he thought about it, the more he came close to a conclusion.

"You are right in the way you are thinking. We know of a very large worm hole existing in the blank space between earth nine and the Milky Way. We could get there by using the veil, but we have to be very careful. It will need the three of us to link ourselves, and not loose touch. Raven will lead us to the primal worm hole. She can only do this because of her ancestor, Martiz. She passed on her channelling capabilities to Ravenna, her mother, but the stress killed her. Raven is more fluid. I need to stress working together and for being careful of what we do. In fact, we have to do exactly what she tells us to do, no matter what. Are you with us?" Titan asked as his eyes seemed to widen, and his pupils grew very large.

It scared Henry to see this. He did not know what to think. One thing for sure, something had to be done. He took a deep breath, "Yes, indeed, I am with you and Raven. I will submit to all that she says."

Raven looked upon his face as if she was trying to figure Henry out. Her head cocked to the left and then to the right, "Yes, Henry, there is a control. This control is so simple that no one, not even the smartest of creatures can figure it out. We can only see it safely, in the way we are now. We can float, fly, move any direction, go to outer space with no need for air. We are only a slip of ourselves within the veil. We must pass through this second arch of turquoise, because the power of the stones themselves will protect us as we journey. Come, let us go to the primal wormhole, creator of all the worm holes, fragments, and filaments. My wish to find out, as we travel is, who created the primal?"

She took Titan's hand, then she took Henry's hand, walking them towards the second archway.

Henry hurt when she grabbed his hand. How could he hurt if he was within the confines of the veil? Looking straight ahead, he could feel himself tremble as they approached the second archway. For a moment, he felt himself drawn to look upward at the arch as they passed underneath. There were words scribed upon the turquoise. They read as such, *"What you see and hear might have a hidden meaning. Listen carefully to all that is spoken to you."*

When they arrived on the other side of the arch, Henry hoped that he had understood all of what was written upon the arch. He looked at Raven, still trying to cope with her dreamlike state. He was then drawn to Titan. The man's countenance unnerved him.

"Hidden meaning," came back to

him. Titan, who had once been human, was changed by the Waddis into the Largess gander goose that sat upon the top deck of Seth's boat. The man thought in two realms, animal and human. Confusing to him, Henry felt that it had a deeper meaning. When Thomasina found him, he was just a newly hatched gosling. Confusing, indeed.

Thomas watched Raven's face as she laid upon the wooden deck of the boat. To him, she looked like she was afraid of something within the realm of the veil. Titan began to waggle loudly. His eyes were closed, yet he waggled so rapidly and loud, Thomasina, who was bringing Thomas a snack, even had trouble understanding him. She handed Thomas his snack, walking over to the gander goose.

"Waaaaagggggglllleee, waaaaaggggglllle," Titan kept repeating. Thomasina knew that in order to understand him, she was to touch him behind each eye. She reached her hands up to the spots she had to touch. Sparks came from his ears as she touched him. No matter what, she had to be in contact with Titan. It did not matter if there was pain. She knew how to block it, as many women do. This was a important matter. Could even be life or death matter. She had to find out.

Thomas was the only one awake. He finished his snack, setting his plate down beside him. Turning his face to the ocean, he looked at it and remembered the good times with Ruby. Tulli and Fannie were sound asleep after their snack. The peeper was curled around Tulli's sturdy little body. Both were content with the food and the company.

Thomasina walked under the first turquoise archway, looking upward to see if there was any writing there. She saw it was blank, only shining green stone, with golden streaks throughout. As she approached the second turquoise arch, she noticed something. There was a very elderly Waddis sitting in the corner of the room. It was actually the corner nearest to the second arch. She walked over to him. She could see, by his legs, that he was taller than any Waddis she had ever seen. His head was shaped almost human, by the way it looked. His long fingers were clasped over his feet, as he sat in the lotus position. She decided to ask him a short question, "Kind sir, do you know of Martiz and her legacy?"

Immediately, his eyes flew open. They were not the pin drop cold eyes of the Waddis, but a very dark brown. He had laugh lines coming from the corner of each eye, stretching several inches on the sides of his head. She could also see that he had hair, which had been shaved off. Not a Waddis, or, at least, a full Waddis.

The man opened his mouth to speak, but nothing came out. He looked very distressed at this. But as he had opened his mouth, she could see that he had no tongue. A regular punishment from the Waddis elite, when you spoke too much.

"I know simple sign language. If you can understand that, then we can communicate. I still have a minute or two to catch up to my niece and her two companions."

The man started to sign, first apologizing that he could not speak. There was something more important on his mind. What he signed next, Thomasina had already expected. He was asking how she knew of Martiz, and if the young lady with the cold black eyes could be a descendant of hers.

"Why yes, she is. Martiz married a man named Kem Pond on earth nine. They had a few children and then the line

of the family expanded. She is the last one
of her kind, unless she is able to pass it on
to any children she might have.
Sometimes it is passed, sometimes not.
But, who are you?"

The man stood up, revealing that he
was truly tall. He pointed to the second
arch, indicating that he needed to pass
through it, in order to save Raven. She
was in dire danger. The man she thought
was Titan is not. Pointing to himself, he
indicated that he was the correct Titan.
He was part of the largess gander goose
that she had tended all these years.
Thomasina took his hand. With a mere
touch of it, she could see that who she
had thought was Titan was not. This man
was the real Titan.

"We must hurry, come with me,"
she said as they passed under the second
arch, finding themselves right behind
Raven, Henry, and the creature
portraying himself as Titan.

"Raven, Henry, do not go any further. This man is not who he says he is! Stay in place all will be resolved!"

Everyone turned around to look at Thomasina and her tall companion. The man that had been portraying himself as Titan, began to shake violently from head to toe. Everyone soon realized that this man or creature, as it were, had taken Titan's place for years. Titan, being the quiet and shy man that he really was, could not pass through the second arch unless someone took him there. It was that way because if two men or creature or Waddis claimed to be the same thing, one would have to be left behind. The Titan that Thomasina had been speaking to was not Titan at all. This creature was referred to a sycophant, or one that wishes to be something else to achieve a goal. His goal was to get into empty space between earth nine and the Milky Way. He did not care about the wormholes, past or present.

His life was within the empty space he had lived, long before he had been marooned within the veil. Since the true Titan would not offer up a fight, hoping that eventually a solution would come.

The solution did come, in the guise of Thomasina, the elder lady who had taken the gander named Titan to raise. His human self was always within the veil, living a half life in the greyness that prevailed there. The counterfeit Titan had managed to fool Thomasina for some time, knowing that there would be a need for her to come through the veil "some day." When that day occurred, like as now, the creature hoped to be released into the space he needed to go to. That was not going to happen. Since the creature had been portraying himself as Titan for so long, he could not change back into is true self. So as he shook, the body known as Titan began to degrade. Soon all that was left of him was a small pile of sparkling galaxy on the floor. He had been made of stardust. When his life ended, he went back to what everyone was before.

Henry breathed a sigh of relief. He had not wanted to follow this creature into space. Feeling that he had no choice, because of Raven. He wanted to keep her safe. He was looking at Thomasina when he blurted out, "What do we do now? What about all that I was told? What about Fannie? The counterfeit Titan told me that she had somehow been transported to the boat for safety. Also, my body, Seth, and Bernis are enclosed within the tree of life in the home world dimension. Is this all true? I hope my friends are not dead or in trouble. My worries are taking me over. Please give me an answer."

Thomasina first looked at Raven's eyes. They were still very black, no white to be seen, taking the real Titan by the hand, and lead him towards Raven.

"Titan, you stay here with Raven, hold her hand. She must always while in the veil, have someone hold her hand. That keeps her tethered to both worlds, the real, and the veil, which could not be explained. Perhaps it could be considered supernatural. As for you Henry, Fannie is safe on the boat. I have heard of a tree of life existing in the home world dimension. For now, we must take all that was said on faith. Remember the writing above us on the second arch? It says, "What you see and hear might have a hidden meaning. Listen carefully to all that is spoken to you." Take it in and understand it, Henry. It might save your life one day. The true Titan is the grandson of Martiz and Kem. He is Raven's ancestor, reduced to living a half life in the veil and within the gander body of the goose Titan. Come, let us join them," The elder lady said as she took Henry's hand, leading him to where

Raven and Titan were standing. Carefully she swept up the stardust in a little bag, handing it to Titan, "You know what to do with this, my friend. Even though the creature passed, at least the last of him will be where he began life."

Thomasina stood there for a moment, thinking what to do. She must get Henry back to his body, so Seth and Bernis can come out of their stupor, and live again. There also must be a way to get to the control of the primal wormhole. Yes, all the creature said was right. His only ulterior motive was to get back to his home. Ah, indeed. Did he live within the blank space or did he live connected with the primal?

First things first. Thomasina took Henry in hand, leading him to a sort of door, or make shift portal where he could go back to his body and his friends. Down she sent him, she hoped in the right place.

Now to Titan and Raven. Titan was needed for his knowledge of the wormholes. His father, Tennif Pond, had helped his parents scribe the star chart. All the star knowledge he gave to his only son, Titan. He was named so because of his great height. Along with the height, he also had a good heart. There were books hidden within the Pond home, where Raven's mother Ravenna grew up. Only a human of somewhat Waddis descent, could find these books. There was no need for them now, they only needed to find the one, the primal. That would be up to Titan.

Thomasina decided to go with them. She felt that she was needed to help with Raven. Her powers were as yet unchecked. Titan would lead them all to the empty space between earth nine and the Milky Way. There, as it had been since time began,was the primal. She hoped that they could find the control, hopefully close to the outer lip of the primal. She walked over to where Raven and Titan were standing. She could see tears of joy in the man's eyes, as he held his great-great-great-great granddaughter's hand. Raven's eyes were still very black. It seemed that you could see the whole universe within them, even the twinkle of starlight, perhaps.

Henry slid down, back into his body. As he came to, so did Bernis and Seth. The three of them were sitting in a rather large notch in the uppermost trunk of the old tree. However, even if it was old, as it was, the tree of life had fresh bright leaves on its branches. There was no fruit, but there looked to be a form of nut, growing from the branch ends. Henry had heard of this tree since he was a child. His mother always told him to never to eat the nuts growing on the tree of life. If you did, you would become part of it, growing into its roots.

So, as Bernis reached for a nut, Henry stopped his hand.

"We are in the tree of life, Bernis. You must not eat any fruit or nut coming from this tree, no matter how hungry you are."

Bernis put his hand down. He had almost picked the nut that his hunger was longing for. He knew henry to be honest and true, so he left it at that.

"How do we get down off of this tree? We are so high in the air that it makes me dizzy," Bernis complained loudly, for the branch he was sitting on was full of knots that hurt his bottom and legs.

Henry stood up in the notch and said, "Here, follow me down. We are not yet done checking home world for all the damage that has been done. Let us stay together, do not stray, my friends. Our very lives depend on this."

Branch by branch, Henry started to shimmy down from the tree. Seth and Bernis followed as best they could. Both men were bigger than Henry, so they had to be more careful with their footing. Foot hold by foot hold they made it down the tree of life. As they stood at the bottom of the tree, they all looked to where they had come from. None of them could see the top of the aged tree. Gauzy clouds hovered around the topmost branches, full of nuts. Bernis wondered why something so beautiful and delicious should be so dangerous.

Chapter Seven

Thomas turned to look at Raven's sleeping face. Thomasina was still locked with Titan. He could see her lips move, but no sound to be heard. He had listened to the Waddis elders speak together in the quiet of the evenings in home world. They spoke that way, so the other Waddis would not pay attention to them. He kept all he had heard in his heart, because there was no one else to make a stand for the elders. One by one, they were found and killed by their own people. Their only crime was speaking the truth. No newly born Waddis in the state nursery were allowed to know of their parents, their secrets, and the finite truth of all creatures. You are born, you live, you learn, you pass it on to your children before you die. That was how life was in the home world dimension, until the new ones were born and changed everything. What a sad place home world was. To execute someone for telling the truth was too hard to bear.

A single tear flowed from Thomas' eye. He looked again at Raven's tranquil face. More tears joined the single one.

Thomasina joined Raven and the human Titan, "Come,let us travel through the third archway, that will lead us to the empty space we need to go to. On the third arch there was writing carved on the turquoise in the front. It was meant to be read before you entered. As Raven stared straight ahead, Thomasina read them out loud, "Follow me through the final archway. This will lead you to the unknown. Remember the unknown is only so until you find it."

Titan nodded his head in affirmation of the words. Raven nodded her head as well, despite her midnight black eyes glistening with starlight. Titan led the way, holding Raven's hand, then, in due course, taking Thomasina's hand to make the triad complete. Together they stepped through the third archway.

All of them were ready to take on whatever was needed to shut the primal down. Perhaps they already had help in hand?

Fannie woke up in a frenzy. She peeped into Tulli's ear, waking him up. Her whiskers vibrated to each peep that was uttered. Tulli, the good dog that he is, took her in a grasping embrace, easing her fears, so she could rest. She licked Tulli's ears until she was tired, exhaling softly to let him know all was well with her. As she settled, Tulli licked her ears softly, until, he too; was tired. Both of them missed their masters, knowing that they must stay together until their return. Tulli let out a low grunt, to let Fannie know that all was right with him. She peeped softly for a few minutes, finally settling down in a happy place with Tulli.

Henry began to lead his friends out of the thick forest. There was not a sound, no birds, which made it wear upon the three comrades. Their fears were heightened because of the rogue fragments, spilling out filaments to hunt and catch. The foreboding was terrible in their skulls.

Slowly, they found their way, able to keep account of any rogue fragments and their wandering filaments. They managed to find their way around the circumspect of the only town in home world. Creeping along a wall, that gave way to a darkened alley, they were lucky to find where the other fragments were. When they were overdeveloped with data, exponentially spreading out all along the main streets of the town. All was quiet here, too. Bodies, Waddis and human, old and young lay strewn all along the streets and other alleys.

Henry held his fingers to his lips, signalling silence to everyone. He wrote a message on a small sheet of paper he had in his pocket, along with a pencil.

It said, *"I think we have seen enough of all the destruction. I do not think anyone survived this event. Follow me, I will take us to my old house. From there we will take ourselves home."* Silently, they turned to get out of the town, down into the forest, past the tree of life.

After they had walked by the tree of life, they made their way into the thickest part of the forest. The trees would protect their way back. The trees and brush seemed to take care of them as they wound their way back towards Henry's old house. Approaching it, Henry could see a Waddis couple, unlike the other Waddis he had seen through his life. The woman carried a small child on her hip. He could tell by the eyes that they were not true Waddis. They both had brown colored eyes, not even close to the bulging eyes of a full Waddis. They had no real color, just the small black iris, protruding out of the eyeball.

Henry let his friends know that they did not look as if they would cause harm. He walked up to them asking, "Where do you all come from? Are you hungry and thirsty? Do you need a place to stay?"

The couple were quite taken aback with Henry's questions. Seth and Bernis knew where he was headed.

The man stepped forward, "We came from the breeder house. All our lives we were trained to take care of the breeders. My mother was a breeder, she had to give me to the Waddis when we were given to them by our people as a peace offering. Some peace offering. They worked us from sun up to sundown, doing all of their dirtiest work. My mother was forced to bear child after child that she never saw after birth. As soon as she gave birth to the babies, the Waddis would take them away to the brooder houses. There they would bring them up in the Waddis way.

It was good that she never saw them again. Most of them were changed to mindless zombies, that worked without rest, or even sustenance. When my mother died, I ran away from the breeder house. For a long time I lived alone by the tree of life. There was a cave near there, no one ever tried to go into. Everyone thought it was haunted, because at night, I would make all kinds of sounds, so they would think it was haunted. One day, I was out hunting for fruit and meat. That is when I met Sarai and her mother. They had the same story as I did. We all decided to live together in the cave. They would even help me at night, making strange sounds. So it worked for a while. Sarai's mother died about three years ago. We decided to go deeper into the trails and denser forests, because the Waddis were getting too close to the cave. We found a place to live quietly, with fruit trees and wild game. Then we heard of the rogue fragments and filaments killing the Waddis, and anything else that stood in its way. We started to see them on the edge of the forest. That's when we took all we had, put it in a wagon I had made, and picked up our child, Merit. We have been walking for days. All I want to do is go back to the cave by the tree of life. Hopefully, we could safely live there until all this chaos died down.."

The man, whose name was David, put a protective arm around his wife and daughter.

Henry's eyes sparkled, "Do not worry, we have people trying to take care of the fragments and filaments at this moment. I grew up in a breeder house like you. I never knew why, but the Waddis gave my mother a little house, where she and I could live. Oh yes, I worked very hard in the data pool, but that is behind us now. I would like to give you and your family this house. There is a running brook in the back, and fruit trees surround the property. You are welcome to have it for as long as you want. It is in a spot unknown to most. If you follow me, I will show you to it. Come, let us go there," Henry said and signalled for all of them, Seth and Bernis as well, to follow him through the tangled brush.

Raven, Titan, and Thomasina stepped upon a flagstone, together. This particular flagstone was one of destiny. Whoever stepped upon it would be able to grasp what they needed to do without harm. The flagstone, with the three upon it, began to float into space. Thomasina was scared at first, but Titan had a sure grip on both of the women. He knew that this mission was up to him, and the women's safety was the same.

Raven, in her shaman state, gazed all around her. She saw planets born. She saw stars collide, and black holes suck up what was left.

Despite the way she was, she could still feel and think. Knowing the primal was their goal, hoping Titan would know exactly what to do to put it to sleep. The big man still had the small bag of stardust that Thomasina had given to him after the star being had perished. He had, in his mind what was to be done. Surely it would come to the end that was needed. Many earths, planets, and dimensions depended upon his choice. Wrongly put, all would perish.

Thomas, once again, gazed out to the sea. His gaze was held by a sight he did not know what to make of. On the horizon, level with the sun as if it were riding on it, was a giant wormhole. If he could see in conjunction with the sun, equal in size, he knew it was big. Terror crossed his heart, making it beat hard. He could feel it like a fist of iron, trying to get out of his chest.

"What could this mean? Is the end of

all worlds coming within my sight? I must pray hard to all that may be. My prayer has got to be heard by everyone than can hear my message," Thomas thought to himself for a minute before he started praying. Then, in one swift move, he got down on his knees, putting his hands together, and began to pray, "To all the powers of good that help us through each and every day. Please let this get to everyone that can hear my message. Pray for your lives and the lives of your children, for there is something so ominous on the horizon that it makes me quake to think about it. I have truly never prayed, ever, so I hope that this prayer of salvation is answered. Great God that watches us all, please provide mankind, and all creatures thereof with an escape from this horror I am witnessing. The Waddis are gone, but their wrath remains in the things that were left behind. Please help us to find a way to overcome what was left to us. I leave my fate within your loving hands."

As Thomas ended his prayer he lifted his gaze, seeing on top of the giant wormhole, three small specks, moving around it. He did not know what the spots were, but he hoped that with his prayer, these things were saving ninth earth from the horror beyond. For sure, he could not know, that everyone on this ninth earth and even on the other earths within the system, were huddled on bended knee, reciting their prayers of hope and sustenance. All of these earths were guided by the same solar star. When it shone its light upon the living, it would make them feel just more so. The darkness was the realm of the dead. No one wished to go there until there time had come. The veil was the only thing that came between life and death. That small splinter of reality that few ever saw.

Thomasina held tightly to Titan's hand. Her other hand held the small bag of star dust from the creature that died creating it.

She knew that the creature might have been the control they were looking for. She was determined to use it now, to rid the universe of this rogue element. Below her, she could see the sun, turning in its own singularity. By the way it was illuminating the primal, she felt that people might be able to see it, and themselves as mere specks. Could that be possible? She thought to herself. She was only too glad that they could not feel the heat of the sun, because they were mere specters of themselves, floating through empty space. She looked up to see the gaping mouth of the primal, oozing fronds of newly made fragments from its huge maw. It made, even her astral self; shudder.

Henry took the little family to see his old house. He showed them through all the rooms. They marvelled that there were actually beds in the bedrooms. They were used to mats on the floor.

He took them out back to show them the fruit trees and the stream. Finally, he showed them the mound where his mother lay, closely covered with all kinds of growing plants.

"Do you like what you see? If you want it, the place is yours to have. My friends and I will be leaving soon, and the house needs someone to care for it."

David looked at Sarai, then to his daughter Merit. Their eyes were aglow with the simple wonderment they had beheld. He turned to Henry, "If you are sure, then we will take care of this place. The sacred mound of your mother will be here to help us too. My wife saw several kinds of edible vegetables growing upon the mound. We would be honored to take care of this wonderful place," he reached out to shake Henry's hand. Henry took his hand and that of his wife, wishing them all the happiness he had growing up here in this small simple place.

"Be kind to it, and it will be kind to you. My friends and I have to leave now, while we still can. So, good luck with your new venture." Henry said and turned to his friends, motioning them to the tree where he had hung the filament. It was still there. Shinning down the gnarled trunk of the tree, he shouted to Bernis and Seth to be ready to hold onto him. When they were all together,tightly holding, he took his flensing knife, reanimating the filament, thinking of Fannie waiting for him, and the happiness he would have when he saw her again. Bernis thought about Raven, and the love he had for her. Seth thought of his parents and his boat. They were ready to go.

Quickly Henry flensed the end of the filament, activating it one last time. Like a cannon shot, they passed right by David and his family, arcing over the dimension of home world.

Death was everywhere. But, where death had been, new life was trying to flower. The tree of life had blooms all over it. The three then passed into the fragment, or what was left of it. Shooting through it until they saw daylight again. Approaching the mouth of the fragment, Henry flensed the filament, closing it permanently. He also did that to all the exposed ends of the fragment. He had to get to the other part of the fragment, to close that down as well, jumping into the clear blue sea, much to the astonishment of Seth and Bernis.

Thomas was watching all this happen, as he stood on the boat. He went and got two strong lengths of rope, heavy enough to carry a man, possibly three men, getting Seth's rifle, which Raven had loaded in preparation for any more need of the weapon. Throwing the ropes out as far as he could, he shouted for Seth and Bernis to take hold of them.

In his heart, he hoped he would remember how to use this weapon, if need be.

Slowly, Thomas towed Bernis and Seth to the ship, until they could get there on their own. Henry was already at the other end of the fragment, flensing and closing off the ends, so it could not wreck anything. He intended to jump back into the water, and swim to the boat. However, he noticed two ridged sharks patrolling the area for more bodies. He would be just a snack for them.

Seth had an idea. He always carried chum fish on the boat to lure fish to his nets. Getting the cannister, opening it carefully, because it would release a foul stench only fish would love. Bernis got out the biggest net, laying it on the side of the railing. Running to the galley, he picked up a dish towel to put the chum, holding the towel while Seth poured some in it.

Tying it up, he secured it within the net, hoping this would work.

With one mighty thrust, Bernis and Seth threw the net as far as they could, to lure the sharks. Thomas already had his ropes ready, throwing them out of Henry to hang onto them. The sharks took the bait, tangling themselves in the numerous knots of the net. Knowing it would not take them long to escape, Thomas pulled with all his might. Bernis came over to help, his strength was phenomenal. Within minutes, Henry was safely aboard the boat. Nothing could have made him happier, other than the little peeper, Fannie. She came running to him, jumping on his shoulder, butting him with her head, peeping, soft, loving peeps for her master.

Tulli came out of the galley to see what was going on, only to find himself within the arms of his beloved Bernis. Raven, Titan and Thomasina were still in their states of unconsciousness. Thomas explained it all. Waiting had to be done, for all three were within the confines of the veil. While they stood there, Thomas pointed out the sun with the giant wormhole on top of it. The black specks were still there.

Thomasina could see a small lump, which was open on one side. She looked into the hole, and found nothing except the debris of a creature that used to live there. Since the lump was on the top of the primal, she took out a handful of stardust, thrusting it into the opening. She then smoothed it down so it made contact with the primal's hood. The three of them stood there, waiting for something to happen.

The primal began to groan. It started to move back and forth. They were safe because they were on the hood of the primal, not making any contact with the main body of the living wormhole. Thomasina decided to put more of the stardust in the lump, packing it down to meet the very tissue of the primal. The primal moaned louder, throwing its head up, moving the hood with it. Titan had already moved the three of them upon the stone to a safe place behind the primal, where it could not see.

"Give me the rest of the stardust, Thomasina."

Handing it over to him, he smiled and said, "Now the two of you must go. After I do this, there will be no room for you or Raven. My body of the veil will disappear, leaving my whole existence within the gander that loves you so. Quickly now, let me step onto the hood, let the stone take you back to the three arches of turquoise. You will be safe there. I love you both," he said after kissing the both of them on their left cheek.

The look within his eyes was one of pure love. No one could forget that.

Thomasina watched Titan walk up the hood of the primal, looking back to check to see if the ladies were out of range. When he was satisfied, he opened the bag of stardust, throwing all of it into the giant searching maw of the primal. He then jumped into the mouth, completely disappearing. Thomasina knew that Titan, the human soul, was gone from the veil. The primal writhed as if in pain, screaming a sound she would never forget. Then she saw it all. The primal slowly shredded into tiny bits, held aloft within the vacuum of space. Soon, all the other worm holes would die, leaving mankind and all its creatures to themselves. She looked at Raven. Her eyes had changed to her own beautiful black eyes. There were tears in them, she knew it was over now. It was time to go home.

Thomas continued to watch over Raven as Thomasina had told him. Tears started to run down the crease between her ears and chin. She started to blink, then opened her eyes as they should, beautiful and black.

"Bernis, Seth, the girl is awake! Praise all that is good beyond us. She has made it through."

Seth stepped aside so he could let Bernis help her up. The connection between these two was very strong, it could be told by the way they spoke to one another, how they held each other, as now. Raven threw her arms around his neck, kissing him on the lips, then the cheeks. She was so happy to see this man. She knew not that he could be the one. She knew that he is the one. Bernis kissed her cheeks as well, both of them glad of their liberation.

Thomasina let go of her hold on the gander Titan.

She now knew that the man that had been, and the gander transformed were one. She could see it in his large brown eyes. A trickling tear fell down his cheek, onto his beak. Thomasina wiped it off with her sleeve.

"Together forever, my dear friend. I am so glad we were all able to come back" she turned around, facing everyone else that was there, "who is hungry?" She shouted for all to hear. A joyous time it was.

After the delicious repast, Thomasina and Raven cleaned up the galley with the help of Thomas. They kept him busy packing what was left of the food they had brought into the packing boxes. Seth and Bernis got the boat ready to move. The sails were unfurled, the anchor was rolled up to the hole it came out of. The rudder was released, because Henry was going to work it.

Seth had already taught him which way to push it when they needed to go a certain way, and, also, to turn. He sat there, in the rudder's chair with his Fannie around his neck. She was busy softly peeping in his ear, and tickling his ears with her whiskers. Fannie loved her master, licking his ears occasionally to make him giggle.

Tulli had found his happy place near to Raven. He knew as soon as she was done helping Thomasina, she would come and get him. Maybe they would ride on the big bird again, he thought to himself. That would be an adventure to him.

Chapter Eight

David and his family marvelled at their good fortune. The rogue fragments had stopped. Died where they sat. No filaments to worry about either. More humans were emerging out of the forest, knowing that the Waddis were no longer, and freedom was theirs for the taking. Everyone was overjoyed at all the beauty that met them as they travelled through the forests in the old home world. There would be no way out of it any longer, but nature would take over, making it easier to live there. Henry had planted one of the nuts from the tree of life behind his old house. It was already shooting up, showing itself to all who viewed it. David and Sarai knew what it was. It was sacred to them, and would continue to be. Merit was fascinated with the plants that grew from the mound where Henry's mother was buried. Happiness seemed to flow from the place to the child, continuing the love of Henry and his mother, for the house, the land, the trees, all of this glorious world where they can live together.

Thomasina packed everything back upon Titan's broad back. She left just enough food for Seth to eat on while he patrolled the boat home. He wanted to be alone for a little while, so he could think about everything that had happened, and what to do next. As it happened, there was no room for Thomas with all that they were taking back. Henry was little, so he was squeezed in between Thomasina and Raven. Fannie, his peeper cat was snuggled into his backpack already asleep in dreams. Raven carried Tulli on her lap, with Bernis behind her on the other saddle. It was his turn to hold on to this lady, who he was growing to love. Behind him were all the packing boxes, knotted and placed where they would endure the quick ride back to the island. To home.

The Piedmonts were coming into view, haloed with thick fluffy clouds, making them a beautiful welcoming present. Henry could not believe his eyes. Home world had never looked like this. Bernis was too busy holding onto Raven, who kept slipping off of the gander's broad back, finally decided to tie her to him, with a spare rope he carried. That way this dear lady was safe on his watch.

Thomasina was singing to Titan. A song she had sung to him when she had first found him. It was about a little duck who got lost from its mother. He waggled along as she sung it to him.

Thomas and Seth got the sails to flowing. They tied the rudder so it would take a straight path to the island. This would not be the singular trip that Seth had wanted to himself. He kind of liked to talk with Thomas. Learning about his life as a Waddis, then his transformation into human. Both of them were glad that Thomasina left plenty of food to do them

until they were back on shore. What was
exciting to Thomas was that as soon as
they would beach the boat, tying it to the
notch up on the beach that was for this
one and only boat. Seth would then flash
a small mirror towards the cottage upon
the Piedmont. In turn, Thomasina would
send Titan, on his own, to pick up the two
men, taking them up to the Piedmont.
Thomas had never been in the air such a
way before. He was anticipating it so
much, that his feet were constantly
wiggling. Seth had to laugh, because, as a
boy, he remembered his first ride on
Titan. He was scared to death of falling
off of the gander, who was as big then as
he was now.

Titan swooped down to the home
turf of the little cottage on the side of the
Piedmont. Gently, he put his webbed feet
upon the familiar land. The mere choice
of it made the great gander waggle with
happiness. He was now happy to be
home, and happy enough to have his

human soul within his gander heart. The world looked much clearer to him now, and he was able to accept his life for what it is.

Soon as Titan was on the ground, Thomasina let the rope ladder down so she could shimmy off of Titan's large back. Henry shimmied down as well, turning his backpack to his front so he could check on Fannie. He could see her little peaked face coming out of the opening, peeping very softly, because she did not know where she was. Soon, she was free of the pack, and busied herself to ride on Henry's shoulders, where she curled around his neck. She craned her neck high to look for Tulli. Peeping loudly for him to answer, she finally saw him still on Titan's back, sitting with Raven. Bernis was trying to untie her from the harness he had fashioned for her. It seemed as if he had tied too many knots. Everyone could hear their laughter on the gander goose.

Finally, everyone was down off from Titan. Bernis had Henry shimmy up Titan's back, dropping the packing boxes. Everyone helped put up all the extra food, pots and pans, and everything else Thomasina though they might have needed on their trip. Everyone wanted to rest under the shade of the fruit trees that were near the cairn. They would visit again some day, but the rest of today was needed for resting, and, of course, eating.

Thomasina figured that near sundown, she would see Seth's flashing signal. That gave her enough time to get a good dinner fixed. She asked Raven to help her. The elder lady could tell that she was very happy.

Titan chose to go to his pen, so he could sleep until he was needed. It felt good for him to be where he called home. Nestling into his large nest, he softly waggled to himself, happy, at last, to be one with his old self and his new self. He could live that way.

Seth and Thomas could almost make out the Piedmonts, ranging high above Toland island. It felt new and good to see the island once again. When they would get to the cottage, he wanted to make sure and ask Thomasina all that they did to rid the relative earths of the wormholes that the Waddis had built. There was no real need for them. When the miners at the seventh earth realized that they would no longer would have to mine the hard ore out of Challaque. The Waddis fled the island, jumping into the ocean, only to be eaten by sharks, who soon turned on them. Preferring to just kill them, and not eat them. What Thomas said was true. there were no real muscles in a Waddis. They were only like a walking brain. The sharks savagely bit into the heads of the fleeing Waddis, instantly killing them. Their bodies sunk into the murky depths. The miners left there were lucky. Not like the others, who died within the rogue fragments.

They would make this place their home. There were others on this earth. Now, these men, *human men;* had a chance to make a life for themselves. Maybe even have a family one day. For now, they hoped to concentrate upon making a settlement. Maybe trying to fish as well. They did see the large expanse of fruit and nut trees. This was an option that would work well. It is now up to the will of the human hosts on the island, rather than the Waddis. If any had survived, they would more than likely go into hiding. Waddis are not good on their own.

Thomasina had just finished tasting the stew, when Raven came running in, announcing that the signal had been made. Seth and Thomas were beached and ready for Titan to come and get them. Asking Raven to wake up the Largess gander goose was not a problem. She grabbed Bernis by the hand, so he could help her wake him up.

They cautiously went to his pen, hearing the soft wagglings of his sleep.

Raven put her hand upon the gander's large eye. She started to rub it softly to wake him up, but there was no need. As soon as he felt her loving hand upon his eye, he woke up, slowly raising his head up. With both of his brown eyes he looked at his beautiful great granddaughter. The human within his soul, hugged her with all his heart. She could feel it, as if the tall man she met within the veil was standing right beside her.

"Come Titan, it is time to pick up Seth and Thomas at the beach. They are ready," Raven said as she stroked his feathered chest. Bernis had already grabbed a saddle to put on Titan's back. As soon as he had it hitched, she hopped upon it, nuzzling her face into the downy feathers at the base of his neck.

Bernis led them out of the pen, then stood back to give them room. With one great flush, Titan was airborne, sailing over the Piedmont towards the coast. As always, the geese in other homes, although somewhat smaller than Titan, hailed his graceful arc across the sky. Raven, snuggled further into his downy neck feathers.

"Titan, from now on I will call you grandfather, because that is what you truly are. I know you will agree, because of the bond and love we have for one another," Raven said and Sighed, digging her hands deep into the down, feeling his skin to hers.

The spirit of Titan the human spoke to her, "My most beautiful grandchild. I will only let you call me this, because it is the truth between you and I. No one else may do this. This is our truth, for the generations that have been, and the generations to come. I love you, Raven."

"I love you too grandfather. No matter how long we live, this will be only ours to share. I am so glad that we found you," Raven said and kissed his ruffled neck, holding tighter as he came closer to the coast.

Thomas was so excited that he couldn't help jumping up and down like a child. Seth watched him enjoying the anticipation for the ride to the cottage. Titan slowly circled around them, spiralling down until his large webbed feet touched the ground. Raven stayed on his back, not wanting to move. She felt so strongly that this might be her last ride for a while, that she just sat there, her hands deep into the downy undercoat surrounding the gander's neck. Seth understood what she was doing,so he let her stay there while he shimmied up the rope ladder she had dropped down, sending a rope down to Thomas to tie to the rest of the packing boxes that they had to take back to the Piedmont.

When all their work was done, Thomas climbed up the rope ladder, lashing himself into where he sat, so he would not fall off. Titan was in flight stance, but did not move. They at last found out the reason. Evangeline was standing just below Titan's large beak. Apparently she was waving to Seth to get his attention. Raven let him know that the lady was there.

"Seth, I would like to invite you to dinner at father Damien's in two days time. It will be for supper. Do you think you can come?" Evangeline asked, looking up at Seth; her cheeks blushing red. Thomas poked him in the ribs to try to get an answer out of him, which made him jump.

"Why yes, I would like to come. Two days from now, at supper? Flash the mirror at the cottage on the Piedmont when it is about time for me to show up. I will bring some of Thomasina'a crusty bread to help with the supper. See you soon!" Seth replied, waving to her as she backed off, giving Titan room to take off.

Thomas poked Seth's ribs again, "That is a right pretty girl. She seems nice, too. It would do you good to get to know her better. I saw how she blushed while she was speaking to you. Undoubtedly, the lady likes you. What harm would it do to pay your respects to her? My Ruby was like that. Shy at first. When I got to truly know her, no other could ever take her place," he wiped the tear that flowed down his chin, snuffling as he did it.

Seth knew that Thomas meant well. He had time now to morn his loss. With that, he could move on with his life. Make something of himself. He turned to Thomas saying, "I have been meaning to ask her out. I always felt that I was too busy. Now I see that there is no time to waste.

Thank you friend, for your kind words,"
he patted Thomas on the leg as he turned
around Raven smiled at her brother.

*"Perhaps he is coming around after
all,"* she thought to her self.

Titan began to waggle loudly as
they approached the Piedmont where the
cottage waited. At first, everyone looked
like ants, running around and jumping.
Soon the view became clearer, and Titan
waggled even louder.

Like a baby's first breath, the
Largess gander goose made a touchdown
on the soft grass of the Piedmont.
Thomasina, Bernis, and Henry with
Fannie around his neck, peeping loudly,
came forward to greet and help everyone.
As soon as Raven was let down, before
Bernis could even kiss her, Tulli jumped
into her arms, wildly licking her face and
Bernis' face. Both brought to laughter
with the little dog's antics. It was a glad
and glorious time.

Thomasina turned to see everyone, with Titan at her back and said, "I am so glad we are here together, safely. I have fixed a wonderful dinner for us all. Seth, show the newcomers how we do it."

Within minutes the dinner was set in the comfortable room within the cottage. Titan and his large pillow was in the center of it all. Even Tulli and Fannie had their own spots, each having their own plate of food. Thomas and Henry gazed at the food, the friends,the animals, and were overcome with thankfulness. Their eyes became glossy with happy tears streaming down their faces.

Thomas stood up, "Dear friends, I would like to say a prayer of thanks for all that we have been through. There is so much to be thankful for, I will try to make it as short as I can," he bent down on one knee, his hands raised to the heavens. Even the animals in the room seemed transfixed with what this man was about to say. At long last, he began to speak;

"For those who watch us from the heavens above, from the divine creator and all his helpers, I give thanks. For all of the people here gathered, I give thanks. For the love shared by all, I give thanks. May we please continue to abide by your peaceful ways. In fact, let us progress in such a way that others can see your works. I give thanks to the heavens above. Amen," Thomas then sat back down, the joy shining on his face.

Everyone began to eat with a reverence for the food before them, the adventures they had survived, and the new things that they had learned. When all was done, Thomasina did not have to ask for help. The help came to her, in the form of all the friends coping with one another, picking everything up, and finally cleaning the kitchen. Fannie and Tulli rested on her lap, tummies full and ready for a nap.

Titan had taken what was left of his plate in his beak, taking it outside for the little birds and chickens to share. When he was done, he handed Raven his plate through the window, kissing her with his large beak. She giggled when he did it. From there, he walked to the shade tree, and sat himself down under it.

When all was finished, it was almost sundown. Everyone went to the little path that led to the cottage and watched the heavenly orb sink down below the waves of the ocean. While there was a small bit of daylight left, Raven, Seth and Bernis went to get the heavy blankets and some pillows. Everyone was sleeping under the stars tonight.

Chapter Nine

Thomasina woke up with a snort. Tulli and Fannie, who had been sleeping with her woke up too. Fannie started peeping very loud, because she did not know where Henry was. He had heard her as he was helping to lay down the heavy blankets on the ground. Running, he stopped at the door of the cottage to see his beloved pet, jump off of Thomasina's lap, leaping onto his shoulder, her whiskers flickering with the intensity of each peep. He carefully took her down off of his shoulders, holding her near his heart so she could hear it. Her peeps grew less and less until they were down to a whisper. Her little head rubbing itself on Henry's shirt. He took her with him then, to see how he could help the others. Soon she was wound around his neck, receiving pretties and pets from all who came near her. Tulli followed, because where ever Fannie was, he wanted to be there too.

Soon everyone was settled on a blanket, looking up at the twinkling stars. Fannie was fast asleep on Henry's chest. Tulli slept beside Henry, keeping watch with one cocked ear, near his new, beloved friend. In fact, Henry was already asleep as well, drifting in dreams of his childhood, running in the forest that surrounded the house he shared with his mother. She was always good to him, teaching him about animals, plants, and how to swim. There were no other children that lived near, and his mother was forbidden to even approach the main city. Somehow they survived, by their own means, and by boxes of food that would arrive at their door every month. Those never stopped, even after his mother passed. He often wondered who brought them. The dreams of now were better and more enjoyable, now that the Waddis had been defeated. Sighing, he entered his dreams again.

Thomas, alone with his thoughts;
lay upon his blanket thinking of his
beloved Ruby. All the wishing in the
world would not be enough to bring her
back. He could pay respects to her
memory by teaching people that hope can
be gained through prayer and meditation.
This was just the same thing Ruby was
trying to teach him, before the Waddis
took her away. Suddenly, he had a
thought that he had not even gone over in
his memory. What if she had been taken
away and not killed? She could be on any
number of earths that the Waddis had
access to. Because of the demise of the
wormholes,fragments and filaments,
there was no inter earth travel any more.
Some one would have to develop a way
of travelling in the space between the
earths. Not by the veil mind you, but by
some other way, just out of reach. "If
only," he sighed before surrendering to
sleep.

Thomasina opted to sleep in her own bed this night. She had missed her bed while they were away. Oh, it hadn't been long, but long enough. She was thankful and glad that all her loved ones got back to the cottage on the Piedmont, safe and sound. It reminded her of a story that her father used to tell her brother and herself in this very same cottage, so many years ago. It was about a little girl who thought she could climb her way up to the stars by a tall tree that was in her backyard. It was a wonderful story, just how did it go? She thought as her head was counting down the numbers until sleep would come.

"Anna and the Way to the Stars,"

There once was a little girl named Anna. In her front yard was a tree so tall, she could not see the top of it. She was always telling her father about this tree, and how it fascinated her so. Her father knew that the tree was none other than a tree of life, which never stops growing throughout all its lifetime. The nuts that grew from the tree were not to be eaten either, or you would become one with the tree forever.

Father always chuckled to himself every time Anna said that she would climb the tree, one day; all the way to the stars. Their life was well enough with their garden and fruit trees. There were also chickens for eggs, and they had two milk cows that Father would milk every morning. The stream behind the little house had fish in it. So, her brother, who was older, would go and fish there for meat for the table. He was very good at it, catching enough for them to dry on racks outside.

Anna's mother became very ill, and the village doctor told them to bare up, for she might not live long. That's when Anna got the idea. She would climb up the tree to the stars, and try to reach God. When she did that, she would speak to

Him about her mother and how necessary it was for her to survive.

One early morning, without telling her Father, she took some of the dried fish, and some fruit; to help her not be so hungry on her visit to God. Anna did not wear her best clothes to climb the tree. She knew that she would get dirty, and snag on things as she climbed up. When she got to the bottom of the tree, she looked up as far as she could. Up her vision went until it could see no more of the great tree, just dense clouds and mist.

With a little sigh, she started to climb up the massive trunk. There were knobbly things all over the bark of the tree, making it easier for her to climb its massive bulk. Climb she did, until she could see the sun almost directly overhead. She knew then it was time to take a break. Anna found a crook in the tree just big enough for her small frame to sit in.

She slowly opened her sack, that had her
snacks in it. First she took out the dried
fish, wrapped in an old, clean piece of
cloth. Dividing the fish carefully, she set
the rest of it on her lap with the napkin
under it. That was when she saw the
movement at her elbow. There was a tiny
brown squirrel with big black eyes,
looking at her. Carefully,the creature put
it's nose forward to smell what she had
on her lap. Well, she knew squirrels did
not eat fish, but she held up a piece for
the tiny thing, so he could, at least, taste
it. Carefully the tiny squirrel smelled the
fish that was offered to him. He put his
paw over his nose, because the smell, to
him; was awful. Anna had an idea. She
put her fish down, reaching into her bag
of goodies. She found two figs that she
had seen in the old fig tree at her house.
Soon the old tree would be full of juicy,
tasty figs. She put both of the figs down
for the squirrel to eat. Again,he carefully
smelled the figs, licking one of them.

He picked that one up, taking a small bite. The juice from the fig, trickled down the squirrel's chin, making Anna giggle. She took out a square piece of cloth she was using as a napkin, carefully dabbing the little brown squirrel's chin. He looked up at her in the utmost of trust and thankfulness. Considering the figs were the squirrel's lunch, the two of them sat there and shared some time together.

Anna woke up with a start, realizing that she had fallen asleep after she ate her meal. The tiny squirrel had curled up in her lap, and was sleeping soundly. She carefully wrapped the remaining fish she had to eat, putting them in her bag. Taking out a small apple from the apple tree at her house, she set it down in the notch she had been sitting in. She had already put the squirrel there as well. Kissing his little furry head, she turned to continue on her journey. She thought to herself as she began to climb, *"I hope that I see that sweet little squirrel on the way down. He is just so precious, being one of God's creatures."*

"Be safe, my little friend," she said as she climbed further up the tree.

The afternoon sun was shining at an angle, making the leaves on the tree shimmer. Anna was not afraid. She was on a mission. The shimmer of the leaves reminded her of her mother, so fragile in life, but so strong in spirit. The strength that she had in the beginning of her climb was slowly leaving her. Her arms began to ache with each move, but she still kept climbing. She was within the clouds at the summit of the tree. They felt like silky fingers touching her face and arms. Somehow, it revitalised her; making her climb even faster. She knew, in her heart, that she was close to God. Anna began to pray out loud. She was not afraid, but she was worried about her father and mother. She had left them a note, to let them know what she was doing.

In her prayer, she wanted to say something about that, "Dear God, please help my parents understand what and why I am doing this. My love for them is so great, I do not wish them to worry. Please help me find You."

As soon as she finished her prayer, she heard a soft, beautiful voice. It seemed to be speaking into her ear. She stopped to listen. It spoke, "Anna, you must hear me. Your journey has been a long one, and your kindness to me will be shown to you in kind. I was that little squirrel in the crook of the branches. You lovingly shared your precious food with me. Sit on this safe place, here within a hole in this tree. It is just big enough for you, my beautiful child."

Anna sat within the hole on the trunk of the giant tree. Looking from above, the clouds had thinned. She was indeed near the top of the tree! The voice continued to speak, "I am here to answer your questions, listen to your worries. It is my job to do this, for I am. What do you need to say to me, child?"

The little girl opened her eyes wide because beside her sat a very big man. Despite his bigness, the air around Him was gentle and sweet. She thought that she could hear singing, only it sounded very far away. Nonetheless, it was beautiful music, and it calmed her to hear it. She looked at the man, knowing full well just who He was.

"First of all, I want to say that I recognize you as God. The air around you tells me that. Now that is off of my heart, here is what I came to ask you about. My Momma has been very ill for a long time. I am so fearful that she will die before long. I have come to ask you for her life to be spared. She is still young, and if you help her, she could live longer, to be with her family. Can you do that for me kind Sir?"

She could hear Him chuckling at her very childlike defense.

"I am not laughing at you. I am remembering my son from a long time ago, he had the same fears about his earthly mother. There is nothing to worry about, child, for her fevers have broke. She is awake and speaking with your father. They are both very worried about you. Your brother has been waiting all day at the bottom of this great tree. Your mother and father will join him soon. They do this because your father forbid your brother to climb up after you. Do not worry, you will make it down by dinner time. Bless you my child, for your heart is big with love, and this will carry you throughout your life, " He said and picked her up, and floated down slowly to the ground. While her brother was there, he did not see Him lay her down against the trunk of the tree, amongst a little mound of leaves to soften her place.

There He left her, to be with her family, and tell of her adventure. This, indeed; would spread His eternal word.

Chapter Ten

Anna woke up with a start. She thought she was still in the tree speaking to Him. There she was, sitting on a mound of leaves at the base of the mighty tree. Her brother had just noticed her, and was calling for their father. But, instead of just her father coming out, her mother and father came out holding hands. The joy of seeing their beautiful daughter standing there before them, made them weep with happiness. Anna ran quickly to their waiting arms. Her brother came over to hug her as well.

"You had us worried, Anna. Did you climb that big tree to the top? You must tell me the truth, my love, so we can all understand why you went up there," Her father was kissing her cheeks as he spoke to her. She knew that he was not mad, just concerned about his precious girl.

"Father, I did climb the tree so I could speak to God about Momma.

When I got to where there were no clouds any more, he appeared before me. He looked like you or me, except a lot bigger. He was so calm and loving when he spoke to me. He assured me that Momma would be all right in no time. Then I woke up down here! But, I do have proof that I was high up there."

Anna pulled a round nut from the tree that could only be found in the topmost branches of the tree. Way past where she had seen the squirrel. Her father took the nut in his hand, knowing what needed to be done. He took Anna by the hand, walking her over to a place to where the growing of this acorn-nut into a monumental tree could be watched from her bedroom window. It was now her place to water the tree, and to let no weeds corrupt its splendour.

Years passed after this day. Anna's parents had grown old together, living in their little house by the two trees of life.

When their time came, they were buried side by side under the first tree. Anna stayed with the house and kept the same bedroom, so she could watch over her charge. The man who became her husband accepted this as well, because he was prayerful and good. Their twin children, both girls; grew up to respect both of the trees.

When it came time for Anna to join her parents and husband of many years ,she was ready. Beautiful singing could be heard all around her. The smell of roses permeated the room she lay in. Her twin daughters were on either side of her bed, when they both heard her say, "Thy will be done." Looking at their mother, her face shone like diamonds. The glow filled her room. It was then the angels came to take her to heaven. Leaving her earthly body on the bed, they lifted up her spirit, arm in arm, taking her up to heaven.

Her twin daughters knew what they had to do. They buried their beloved mother by their father, under the second tree of life. When they did this, nuts fell from the tree. It was time to do more planting.

Thomasina sighed in her sleep. The story had rested her spirit and eased her mind. She fell into a deeper sleep, dreaming of the days when she was a child on the Piedmont.

Bernis and Raven had talked long into the night. When the moon was high in the sky, they had both fallen asleep on the great blanket under the stars, but not before pleading to go and investigate the old Pond cottage after breakfast. It was Raven's anyway.

Henry sighed in his sleep. Tulli had joined Fannie, both sleeping deeply on Henry's chest. The warmth of their little bodies made Henry all the more comfortable with their infinite love.

Seth's dreams were colored with Evangeline, speaking to him over a dinner table. In his heart he knew that she was *"the one."* He just had to convince her of that. Funny, though, his dream also contained children, happy and healthy, sitting with them at the dinner table.

What had happened to all of them was a work in faith. Faith to one another, faith to the God that rules us all,despite what we call ourselves. The gift of promise is the greatest gift, and can be given at any time.

Oh, by the way; Henry did plant the nut from the tree of life behind the cottage on the Piedmont. Everyone put a part of themselves within the hole that was dug. Bernis put a button from the shirt that Raven had given him to wear, Thomas put a small penny whistle that he had somehow saved from the ravages of the Waddis. It had been Ruby's. Seth put an old bent net mending needle that had been his father's. Raven put a lock of her lustrous black hair. Thomasina put a piece of paper on which she had written Anna's story. Henry put a river stone, one of two he always carried. It was smooth and round from being in the water for so long. Last but not least, Fannie peeped loudly as she put a choice bit of mouse she was saving for Henry. Tulli slipped a chew stick he had loved ever since he was a puppy. All that love that was entered into the hole with the seed helped it, I believe. Growing rapidly in the rich soil of the mountain, the tree would grace anyone or thing that gazed upon it. Maybe there will be more of this magnificent tree at a later date. Time will tell.

Earths can come and go. There might be others that can be visited. We need to push the discovery.

The End

Teacher and historian, Sandra Warren is also an author who writes introspective stories from the heart. Half Men being her first literary work, she continues to push the threshold past the boundaries for new and unexpected worlds to explore.

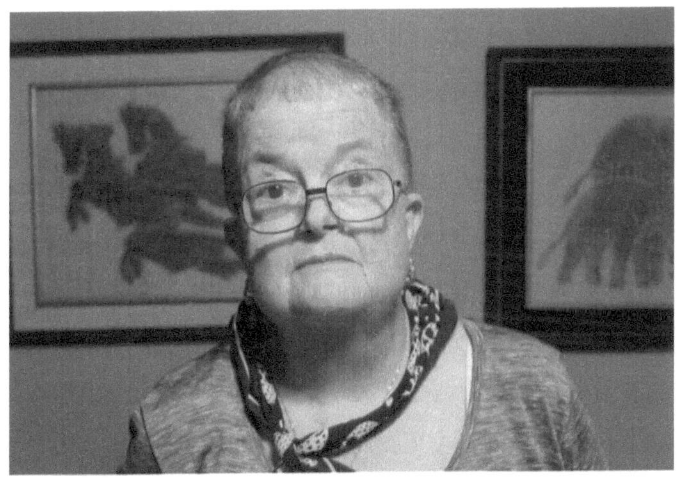

© 2020 Half Men by Sandra Warren. All Rights reserved.

No part of this book may be produced or transmitted in any form or by any means, electronic or mechanical, including copying, recording, or by any information storage and retrieval system without express permission from the author.

This is a work of fiction. Names, character, places and incidents are either the product of the author's imagination or are used fictitiously. Any resemblance to actual events, locales, or persons, living or dead, is entirely coincidental.

www.ingramcontent.com/pod-product-compliance
Lightning Source LLC
Chambersburg PA
CBHW031247160726
47993CB00001B/62